DOUBLE IDENTITY

DOUBLE IDENTITY

MARGARET PETERSON HADDIX

Simon & Schuster Books for Young Readers

New York London Toronto Sydney

SIMON & SCHUSTER BOOKS FOR YOUNG READERS

An imprint of Simon & Schuster Children's Publishing Division

1230 Avenue of the Americas, New York, New York 10020

SIMON & SCHUSTER BOOKS FOR YOUNG READERS is a trademark of Simon & Schuster, Inc.

Book design by Greg Stadnyk

The text for this book is set in Photina.

Manufactured in the United States of America

10 9 8 7 6 5 4 3 2

Library of Congress Cataloging-in-Publication Data

Haddix, Margaret Peterson.

Double identity / Margaret Peterson Haddix.—1st ed.

p. cm.

Summary: Thirteen-year-old Bethany's parents have always been overprotective, but when they suddenly drop out of sight with no explanation, leaving her with an aunt she never knew existed, Bethany uncovers shocking secrets that make her question everything she thought she knew about herself and her family.

ISBN-13: 978-0-689-87374-4 (hardcover)

ISBN-10: 0-689-87374-3 (hardcover)

[1. Cloning—Fiction. 2. Identity—Fiction. 3. Secrets—Fiction. 4. Aunts—Fiction.] I. Title.

PZ7.H1164Be 2005

[Fic]—dc22   2004013448

In memory of Katie
Kristen
Richard
and many others who are gone.

Acknowledgments
With thanks to Dale E. Williams Jr., Robert Ruth, and
Rebecca Harty for their assistance in researching this book.

—ONE—

My mother is crying.

She is trying to do it silently, but from the backseat of the car I can see her shoulders heaving up and down, her entire body racked by sobs. I look out the window at the darkness flowing past our car, and all the pinpoints of light on the horizon seem far, far away. My mother always cries, now. In the beginning, back in the summer, I used to try to comfort her, used to ask her—stupidly—"Is something wrong?" And she'd force her face into some tortured mask of fake happiness, her smile trembling, her eyes still brimming with tears: "Oh no, dear, nothing's wrong. Would you like some milk and cookies?"

That was before today, before my father hustled the three of us into the car and we drove for hours and hours across unfamiliar states, the light fading and the roads we are on getting smaller and smaller, more and more remote.

I do not know why my mother is crying. I do not know where we are going.

I could ask about our destination, if nothing else. A thousand times today I've started to open my mouth, started to squeak out, "Can you tell me . . . ?" But then I'd look into the front seat, at my mother's silent shaking, my father's grim profile, the mournful bags beneath his eyes, and all the questions I might ask seemed abusive. Assault and battery, a question mark used like a club. My parents are old and fragile. I'd have to be heartless to want to hurt them.

A red traffic signal flashes overhead, and my father comes to a complete stop and stares at the empty crossroads for whole minutes before inching forward. He's an insanely careful driver. My mother is too—or was, before she started crying all the time and stopped doing anything else.

I turn my head, looking away from both my parents. We're on the outskirts of a small town now. I squint out the window at a dark sign half-hidden in bushes: WELCOME TO . . . It's S— something, something—field, the letters in the middle covered by branches. Springfield? Summerfield? I've lost track of what state we're in. Indiana? Illinois? Could we possibly have crossed over into Iowa? Maybe one of those I-states has a cluster of seasonal villages I've never heard of: Springfield, Summerfield, Winterfield, Autumnfield. Maybe Mom and Dad are just taking me on yet another educational field trip, like when we went to the Liberty Bell and Independence Hall.

I can't quite believe this, but the thought cheers me up a little. Even educational field trips are better than sobbing and grimness.

A row of fast-food restaurants glows on the other side of my window, and this cheers me too, even though I'm not hungry. Wendy's, McDonald's, Burger King, Taco Bell—so well lit, so safe, so sane, so ordinary. I'm so busy wallowing in the comfort of their garish lights that I almost miss hearing the first words spoken in our car in hours.

"Those are new," my father murmurs.

I glance again at the golden arches outside my window. Nothing looks particularly new to me. But . . . has my father been in this town before?

My mother doesn't answer him. Still, I peer out the window with renewed interest. In a matter of minutes, we come to a town square, with a soaring courthouse and a quaint row of shops. The shops are closed, their signs dark. Spring/Summer-field has gone into hibernation for the night or the winter or maybe even the entire century. Our headlights throw a brief glow on a flaking-away billboard on the side of a building, and I could swear part of the sign is still advertising a circus from 2006. Years ago.

My father turns onto a residential street, turns again, then once more. He pulls up to the curb and shuts off the engine in front of a dark house surrounded by huge trees. The sudden silence is horrifying, and it seems to catch my mother off guard. A tiny whimper escapes her, the sound amplified in the stillness. Surely my father hears her now; surely he and I can't go on pretending she isn't crying.

"Wait here," my father says. He does not look at Mom or me. He gets out of the car and gently shuts the door. He stands still for a second, looking at the house. Then he opens the wrought-iron gate and walks slowly toward the front door.

The streetlights illuminate little more than a square or two of sidewalk, so I can barely see my father as he hobbles up the porch steps. I squint. I imagine that he is pressing a doorbell now, maybe tapping lightly on a screen door. All I can hear is my mother gulping in air in the front seat. Her shudders are practically convulsive now. I reach out, planning to put a comforting hand on her shoulder. But before I can touch her, she plunges forward, burying her face in her hands, sobbing harder.

I pull back.

Up on the porch, a light clicks on, warm and bright and startling after all the darkness. I can see everything on the porch now. It's enormous, wrapping around the entire front of the house and the sides as well. Sometimes I play a game where I pretend I'm a movie set designer: This porch would fit very well into one of those heartwarming family dramas set in the early 1900s. I can picture a dozen children dressed in lacy dresses and knickers lounging on all the white wicker chairs, whiling away long summer afternoons playing marbles and checkers, whispering innocent secrets, laughing at innocent jokes.

That porch is a happy-looking place, and my father—burdened, stoop-shouldered, cadaverously thin—doesn't seem to belong on it.

The door opens and a woman appears. I can't see her face very well, but she has white hair and is wearing a plush red dressing gown. Or robe—I know it's just an ordinary robe, but I've gotten into that old-fashioned mindset. The woman surprises me by stepping out onto the porch and throwing her arms around my father. He stands there awkwardly, like he's not sure he wants to be hugged. He glances back anxiously toward our car, toward Mom and me.

The woman releases him from the hug but still keeps one

hand on his arm. She says something I can't hear. I glance toward the front seat again, where my mother still has her face buried, trying not to hear or see anything. I reach over and grip a knob on the door beside me. We are the only people I know who still have manual controls for rolling our car windows up and down. This is a fairly new car—only a year old—so my dad must have asked for the nonelectronic controls special. Maybe he even paid extra. Usually I'm embarrassed that my parents are so low-tech, but tonight I'm grateful. I roll down the window in total silence.

My father is answering the woman.

"Oh, Myr," he chokes out. "I hate having to ask this of you. . . ."

He glances toward the car again, and I crouch down into the shadows, hoping it's too dark for him to see whether a window is open or closed. The woman pats his arm, cradling her hand against his elbow.

"You know I'd do anything for you and Hil," she says. I like her voice. It's throaty and rich, and if I were pretending to be a movie director instead of a set designer, I'd cast her in my historical drama as the wise old governess, or maybe the kindly housekeeper.

"You'd do anything?" My father repeats numbly. "Even now? After—?"

"Even now," the woman says firmly.

My father makes a garbled noise and then he begins sobbing, clutching the woman against him, weeping into her shoulder. Unlike my mother, my father does not cry quietly. His wails roll out like a wave of pain, and I scramble to roll up my window. My mother cannot hear that. I cannot bear to hear it myself. I am not used to my father's crying. I've had no time to harden my heart against him.

I sit still for a few minutes, breathing hard, staring at the back of my mother's seat. *Crazy, all this is crazy. Why didn't they just let me go to school today, like usual?* I latch on to that one word, "usual," and let it float through my mind a few more times. I call out its brother and sister words and form a comforting litany. Usual. Ordinary. Normal. Safe. Sane. Typical. Sane, safe, typical, ordinary, usual, normal.

My parents have never been normal. . . . That's a traitorous thought, and I hunt it down and stomp it dead.

I glance back at the scene on the porch, and I'm relieved to see that my father has gotten control of himself again. He's not clutching the woman in the red robe anymore. They're not even touching, just talking earnestly. I roll down my window again.

At first, their voices are indistinct—it's like they're trying not to be overheard. I hear my own name once or twice: "Bethany is . . . Bethany does . . . ," but the rest of the sentence is always lower-pitched, and I can never tell what my father thinks I am or do. Then the woman asks something and my father shakes his head violently, vehemently.

"Oh, no," he says, loud enough for me to hear, loud enough for me to be sure of what he's saying. "She doesn't know anything about Elizabeth."

Elizabeth? I think. Something about the name or the way he says it stabs at me. Whoever she is, Elizabeth is important.

My father is still shaking his head, and the woman gives her shoulders a slight shrug.

"All right, then," she says.

"Thank you," my father says. He retreats from the woman and the light beaming out from her porch, and I think, *That's it, now we can go home.* But I barely have time to roll up the window before my father's standing beside the car, leaning down, opening my door.

"Bethany, honey?" he says, and his voice is all wrong—too hearty, too cheerful, too fake. "We're going to let you stay with your aunt Myrlie for a while. What would you think of that?"

Aunt Myrlie? I think. *Aunt?* I thought all my parents' brothers and sisters were dead. I thought my family was just Mom, Dad, and me.

My father doesn't wait for my answer. He's hunched over the trunk now, pulling out a suitcase. Just one. Mine.

This is crazy, because I am twelve years old, almost thirteen, but I've never spent a single night away from my parents. I've been invited to sleepovers, of course, but there was always some reason my parents had to come and pick me up early—I had a swim meet the next day, my mother didn't want me tired out for school, it just wasn't a good time. . . . Three of my friends went away to camp last summer, and I asked to go too, but I didn't ask very persistently because I knew what the answer would be, the same one I always got: *No. Maybe another time. When you're older.* I'd thought "when you're older" was just code words for "never," but here my father is, plunking my suitcase down on the sidewalk. It sits there looking alone and abandoned, and my father moves back to my car door to see why I haven't gotten out.

"Bethany?" he says.

"I have a social studies test tomorrow," I say. "First period."

And that's a ridiculous thing to say, because even if we drove all night, we wouldn't be home in time for me to make it to school first period. But I guess all day long, as I watched my mother cry, as I watched the unfamiliar landscapes fly by, I'd been holding on to the notion that however strange today was, tomorrow would be normal again, just another ordinary school day.

"Bethany," my father says again, and some of the fakeness has chipped away and I can hear the ache in every syllable of my name. "You have to stay here so I can get help for your mother."

The emotion in his voice is completely raw now. I wince, the way I would if I were staring at an open, gaping wound. I could ask plenty of questions—*Where are you planning to go to get help for Mom? Why didn't you just have me stay with one of my friends back home? Who's this Aunt Myrlie, anyway? Who's Elizabeth?* But I can't even bear to meet my father's eyes.

I get out of the car.

My father circles around to the front and opens my mother's door.

"Hillary?" he says, too loudly. "We're here. It's time to say good-bye to Bethany."

Dad motions for me to come and stand next to him. So I'm there in time to see Mom staring dazedly out of the car.

"Nooo," she wails. And then she hurls herself at me, and wraps her arms around me so tightly I can barely breathe. I am taller than my mom now—I grew seven inches in the past year—and it crosses my mind that my height may be the only thing saving me from suffocation.

Mom buries her face in my shoulder, and I put my arms around her. But she's weeping so hard it's like trying to hold on to an earthquake. Her sobs shake us both. She won't let go until my father peels her hands off me.

"I'm sorry," he says, and I can't tell if he's apologizing to me or to her. She collapses back into the car and he leads me away. He retrieves my suitcase, he holds the gate open for me, we climb the porch stairs—all of it feels like a bad dream. Maybe that's why I'm so docile, so obedient. In dreams you don't have choices, you just do what you do, and in the morning you comfort yourself with the idea that none of it really happened.

The woman—Aunt Myrlie?—gasps when I come into the light.

"Bethie?" she breathes incredulously. "Oh, Bethie—"

"It's Beth*a*ny," I correct her, irritably. But I don't think she hears me because she's bounding across the porch and throwing her arms around me in total joy. I hold myself stiff, partly because she's a complete stranger and partly because I've just been released from my mother's sorrow-wracked hug and it's too much of a jolt to go from that to this spontaneous burst of delirious happiness. After a few seconds the woman releases me.

"Sorry," she mutters. "I forgot myself. You just look so much like . . ." She glances quickly at my father and lets her voice trail off.

"You see how it is," my father says gruffly.

The woman nods silently and now there are tears in her eyes too.

"Come on in," she says, holding the door open for us. I step across the threshold but my father doesn't follow. He looks down at the strip of metal dividing the wooden floor of the porch from the wooden floor of the foyer as if it's electrified and deadly. Or as if, once he crosses it, he can never leave again.

"I really should be going," he says, glancing back at the car and at Mom.

I step back toward my father. I've spooked myself thinking about dangerous, uncrossable doorways, and even though I am nearly thirteen I have to fight the urge to throw myself at my father's feet and wrap my arms around his legs and beg like a little child, "No, please, Daddy, don't go."

My father hands me my suitcase, like he knows what I want to do and that's his way of stopping me.

"You'll be fine with your aunt Myrlie," he says, the fake heartiness back in his voice. "And we won't be gone long."

"Will you be back for my birthday?" I say forlornly. I don't know why I ask that. My birthday is November 2, still more than a week away, and the question really does make me sound like a child. It's just that birthdays are a big deal in my family, and I'm not sure I can bear it if my parents are away then.

I fully expect my father to say, "Yes, dear. Of course we'll be back long before your birthday. With lots of presents." But I look up and my father is staring back at me in mute horror. He opens his mouth, but no sound comes out. He reaches out and brushes his fingers against my cheek, cradling my face in his hand. And then his hand slips away and he stumbles off the porch, down the walkway, back to the car. He moves like he's drunk, though he couldn't be. He's barely even eaten today, let alone had anything to drink. And I've been with him for the past fifteen hours. I would know.

Really, except for school, I've spent virtually every second of my life with my parents. How could I not know what's wrong with them?

How could they be leaving me now?

—TWO—

"Well," the woman says.

I'm still staring off after my parents' taillights, staring at empty street. I've practically forgotten the woman is there. No—Myrlie, I remind myself. Aunt Myrlie. But I've never called anyone "aunt" before, so the name feels strange to me.

I won't call you that, I think defiantly. *I won't.*

Still, I tear my gaze away from the darkness where my parents used to be and glance at Myrlie. Up close, she doesn't look so old, despite the white hair, despite the Mrs. Santa Claus robe. Her face has surprisingly few wrinkles, and her dark eyes are brimming with sympathy.

"Are you hungry?" she asks. "Would you like something to eat? I don't keep much food in the house, seeing as how it's only me living here now, but I'm sure we could scare up something. Peanut butter and jelly sandwich, maybe? Chicken noodle soup? Or—?"

"I'm not hungry," I say. Then, because some of my defiance has leaked into those three words, I add, "No, thank you."

"Okay," Myrlie says evenly. But she doesn't seem to know what to say to me if she can't talk about food. She can't even look me straight in the eye. It's as if I'm hideously ugly, painful to look at, and I don't think I am. I've got long blond hair that I once described in a school essay as "cascading down my shoulders"—my teacher took off points for that because he said it was an overwrought cliché. And, truthfully, my hair doesn't really cascade. It just kind of lies there.

I also wear narrow, brown-rimmed glasses. My mother started bugging me a couple years ago to get contacts, but I like my glasses. My face would feel naked without them. Unprotected.

Is that why my mother started crying? Because I fought with her about glasses? Is it all my fault?

I can't let myself think about that right now, or else I might start crying right here in front of Myrlie. I force myself back to evaluating my appearance. Before I grew seven inches in the past year, everyone always said I was tiny and cute. I don't think I'm any less cute for suddenly growing tall, but people can probably tell by looking at me that I'm not used to being this height yet. I like to collect unusual words (hence, "cascading" and, well, "hence"), and the word I like to use about myself is coltish. So what if I'm a little wobbly on my legs right now— someday I'll race the wind.

Anyhow, "tall and coltish" sounds a lot better than "tall and gawky," which is probably a more accurate description.

Somehow I've survived two or three minutes of this strange

woman staring at me without quite looking straight at me. But thinking about my appearance can last me only so long.

"Um," I say. "Maybe I can use your phone?"

I feel brilliant suddenly—why didn't I think of this sooner? I'll call my dad's cell phone and just tell him how ridiculous everything is. I don't want to stay here, he and Mom didn't want to leave me behind, Myrlie doesn't seem to know what to do with me—so let's just undo everything. And he'll come back and pick me up and we can all go together to get help for Mom.

This is virtually the same plan that got me out of attending the first three months of first grade, but I don't care about seeming childish anymore. I'm picturing Mom and Dad and me riding off into the sunset together (or toward sunrise, anyway).

Then I see the turmoil my question has unleashed on Myrlie's face.

"I don't think . . . ," she begins, stops, starts again. "Look, I know this is probably all very strange for you. It's strange for me, too. I feel like if I forbid you to use the phone, it'll seem like you're trapped here. Like I've kidnapped you, or something. When actually . . ." She lifts her hands helplessly, as if explaining exactly why I'd been dropped at her doorstep is far beyond her verbal abilities. "Walter said it was very important that you shouldn't try to contact anyone."

"I just want to call him," I say, and it's all I can do not to make my words a whimper: *I want my daddy* . . .

"Well . . ." Myrlie wrinkles her brow, deliberates. Somehow in that moment I decide I like her. She's taking me seriously. "I don't see how that could be a problem."

I follow her down a hall and into a kitchen, but I don't pay much attention to any of it. Why should I, if I'm just going to leave again in a few minutes?

The phone is on the kitchen counter, and it's an old-fashioned landline, actually connected to the wall with a cord. I punch in the familiar number and put the phone to my ear. I hear one ring and a click and then a computerized voice: "We are sorry. This number is out of service."

"What?" I say out loud. I've known my father's phone number since I was four, but I must have misdialed. I hang up, then pick up the phone again and push the numbers with exaggerated care. This time I check the number on the phone's digital screen: 484-555-9889. Yes.

I lift the phone to my ear again—ring, click, computerized voice: "We are sorry. This number is out of service."

I'm starting to panic. I try my father's number again; I dial my mother's number, even my own, though my phone broke yesterday, and that's why I don't have it with me now. (And *why* did my phone break right before this bizarre trip? Was it just a coincidence? Or . . . not?)

Out of service.

Out of service.

Out of service.

I call the nationwide directory and ask for any listing for a Walter, Hillary, or Bethany Cole, hometown, Greenleaf, Pennsylvania.

"Checking, checking," the computerized voice says. Then, "We are sorry. We have no listing for any of those names."

It's as if my family ceased to exist. As if we never existed. I collapse against the kitchen counter, let the phone drop from my hand. There's not even any real live human I can argue with, protest to.

I feel a gentle hand on my back. I've forgotten about Myrlie again. She's been standing here the whole time, listening to every word.

I turn to face her.

"Isn't there any emergency number my father left with you?" I choke out. "Some way to reach him if I break my arm or, or . . . ?" My throat closes over my next words. I can't say them. *Or if I just need him?*

Myrlie's eyes are filled with fear now. Fear and confusion and something I can't quite read.

But slowly, slowly, she shakes her head no.

—THREE—

Myrlie tucks me in to bed. I go along with her, as compliant as a rag doll. She carries my suitcase to an upstairs bedroom, helps me pull out my pajamas, helps me slip them on. And I don't care that this stranger sees me half-naked, don't care that she's treating me like a five-year-old. My brain doesn't start functioning again until she's pulled the down comforter up to my chin and turned out the light and murmured, "Things will look better in the morning. They always do." Then, when I'm lying there, wide awake in the darkness, some tiny, tiny part of my mind comes alert again to goad me: *You're overreacting.*

Except, I'm not. It'd be one thing if my parents were like the adults I've seen dropping their kids off late for school or smacking their toddlers in the grocery store or growling at their teenagers at the mall, "Stop bugging me!" If I belonged to any of those parents, I wouldn't be all that surprised to be foisted off on a stranger in the middle of nowhere, with no way to reach my mom and dad.

Okay, maybe I'd be surprised, even then. It's just a million times worse because my parents are the most careful, over-protective, parentish people I've ever seen.

Even when I was little, they never hired a baby-sitter for me. When I was four or five—probably five, after I'd watched Gretchen Dunlap across the street go off to kindergarten while I was being home-schooled—I somehow got wind of the fact that other kids sometimes had babysitters who let them jump on the couch cushions and eat all the cookies they wanted and even go to bed without brushing their teeth. I wanted that too, so I asked my parents for a babysitter of my own. I remember my parents looking sad—disappointed, maybe, even hurt— and then my mother bent down on her knees in front of me and said, "Oh, honey, why would we want to spend even a second away from our baby? You don't need a sitter. You've got us. All the time. Always. Forever." She even agreed to let me jump on the couch and eat too many cookies and skip brushing my teeth every once in a while. But somehow I knew it wasn't the same.

And when my parents take me to the mall, they don't go to the boring stores and make me sit and wait while they pick out vacuum cleaners or refrigerators or ties or anything for them-selves. They sing out, "This shopping trip is all about you!" And even when we're loaded down with bags of jeans for me and sweaters for me, and new DVDs for me, they still beg, "Isn't there anything else you want us to buy?"

The last time we went on one of those shopping trips, I spent the whole time whining, "You're embarrassing me," and, "Stop being so loud," and, "Nobody else I know has to stick with her parents the whole time at the mall."

Guilt surges through me as I'm lying there in the bed in Myrlie's house. It feels like the ceiling has opened up and a huge bolt of guilt-lightning has zapped me.

Oh, no. What if my parents know how ungrateful I am and this is their way of teaching me a lesson?

I close my eyes and I can hear voices echoing in my head: Gretchen Dunlap from across the street telling me, "*My* mom says you're the most spoiled kid she's ever seen. So there!" when we were five or six. And my snarling at my mom, "You're driving me crazy! Just leave me alone!" after she'd offered to braid my hair when I was nervous about a swim meet.

That was before she started crying, I tell myself. *I wasn't mean to her after she started crying. Why would they drop me off in this strange place and then vanish* now?

And then I feel almost disappointed, because my parents doing this to teach me a lesson would be strange, but sort of understandable. Without that explanation, I've got nothing.

Maybe none of this has anything to do with me, I think, and that's a big leap for me. My parents have spent my entire life telling me how important I am, how much they love me, how everything in their lives revolves around me. *Maybe things changed,* I think. *Maybe now I'm just . . . in the way.*

I swallow a lump in my throat, but I can't believe this explanation either. Even a long, long time ago, before she became a permanent fountain of tears, I can remember my mother looking at me and starting to cry, just out of the blue. And the past several months, my father has seemed much more worried about me than about my mother—it's my seat belt he double-checks every morning when they drive me to school, it's me he follows in the car when I'm out rollerblading around the neighborhood. (Which is why I pretty much stopped rollerblading around the neighborhood.) Then there's the way Myrlie reacted when she saw me. She was so happy at first—and then it seemed like it broke her heart just to look at me.

Why? I think. *Why, why, why, why, why?*

It's that word that carries me off to sleep, a lullaby of curiosity and loneliness and fear.

—FOUR—

In the morning I wake up disoriented. I can't quite believe I made it through the night, all by myself, so far from home. Sunlight is streaming in the windows past white, dotted swiss curtains, and in spite of myself I'm a little pleased that I can put a name to the thin, old-fashioned material.

It's a shame it's not dimity, I think, just because I like that word better. I'm not actually sure what dimity looks like.

I am the only kid I know who's even heard of dimity, who likes old-fashioned words, who's ever bothered to read the dusty, falling-apart books at the back of the school library, behind the brand-new computers. I think it's because my parents gave me so many antique toys when I was little, along with the Bratz dolls and the toy computers. I'm the only kid I know who had a Cabbage Patch doll; I was the only one who had a collection of *My Little Pony* videos and my own VCR, instead of just DVDs and a DVD player.

Thinking about my old toys makes me sad, and I get an ache in my throat that makes me want to be a little kid again just so I can get away with throwing myself on the floor and pounding my fists and hollering, "I want my mommy! I want my daddy! I want to go home!"

Instead, I make myself sit up and put on my glasses so I can look around.

I'm in one of two twin beds angled on one side of a spacious room, opposite a wallful of windows. Both of the beds are covered with lacy yellow comforters, and the furniture is all white, even the desk that's under the windows. It's clearly been a little girl's room, and that makes me wonder about Myrlie. "It's only me living here now," she said last night. Did she used to have a husband? Kids? Myrlie is a mystery to me—the only thing I know about her is that my father said she was my aunt. Does that make her my father's sister or my mother's?

It bothers me that I don't know this, but my parents never talked much about their own childhoods. For all they've told me about their pasts, you would think their lives began the same day as mine.

I slip out of bed and cross the room to one of the windows. It looks out on a generous backyard studded with huge, brightly colored trees. Two at the back particularly stand out: one bigger, one smaller, both brilliant red. The autumn leaves surprise me, because when we were driving yesterday, right up until nightfall, all we passed were bare, bleak landscapes with trees holding empty branches up to a gray sky.

You've come south, I tell myself, and I'm proud of my powers of deduction. *Trees lose their leaves later the farther south you* go—ergo, *Myrlie's house is a good deal south, as well as west, of Greenleaf, Pennsylvania.*

But this reminds me that I don't even know what state I'm in, and I don't feel much like gloating over my brilliance.

I wander around the room aimlessly, fingering a miniature glass tea set on the dresser, a china doll on the desk. Since I've never stayed the night before at anyone else's house, I'm not sure what the rules are. Am I supposed to wait in the room until Myrlie comes to get me? Or am I supposed to go downstairs so she knows I'm awake?

Trying to decide, I open the door and peek out into the hall. I catch a glimpse of a sink and a toilet behind a nearby door, and I decide that no one could fault me for going to the bathroom. The bathroom is an old-fashioned one, with claw feet on the bathtub and a black-and-white tile floor and separate knobby handles on the hot and cold faucets. If I concentrate really hard, I can distract myself from the weirdness of my situation by thinking about how this bathroom could fit in the early-1900s movie I was imagining the night before. But bathrooms don't usually figure very prominently in those kinds of movies, so I'm still feeling strange and awkward and uncomfortable when I open the door.

Myrlie is climbing the stairs, right outside the bathroom.

"Good morning!" she says, with some of the fake heartiness my father employed last night. "I thought I heard you stirring about up here. I didn't know if you were an early riser or someone who could sleep the whole morning away like . . ."—she freezes, looks a little panicked, then hastily continues—"like a lot of kids. Anyhow, since you got to bed so late last night, I thought I'd just let you sleep until you woke up. Although, with the time change, you're probably totally messed up. I took the day off work so I'd be sure to be here when you got up. Would you like some breakfast?"

She's doing that thing where you talk too much when you don't know what to say. I tend to go in the other direction—not talking enough—so I stand there for a few seconds in silence. *Am I in a different time zone now?* I want to ask, and, *Who is it that can sleep the entire morning away—besides me?* But all I say is, "Breakfast would be nice."

I follow her down the stairs and she offers me bacon and eggs and toast—"Or pancakes? How about pancakes?" I choose Raisin Bran, the only cereal in the house. It's the kind of breakfast I wouldn't touch back home—Froot Loops are more my style—but somehow it seems like I'd be even more beholden to Myrlie if she went to the trouble of scrambling eggs or mixing pancake batter, just for me. I feel strange enough ladling the cereal up to my mouth and chewing and swallowing while Myrlie sits across the table watching me.

Suddenly I'm disgusted with my own wimpiness, my willingness to sit there as meekly as a lab specimen under a microscope when I've got so many questions swarming through my mind.

I swallow hard and the Raisin Bran scrapes down my throat.

"Where do you work?" I ask, because it seems like a nice, neutral opening shot.

Myrlie jumps a little, like she's forgotten I have a voice. Or like she thinks that's something I should already knew.

"Oh!" she says. "At the school. I teach kindergarten."

I can see her as a kindergarten teacher, all cheerful and

patient and, "Now, let's try 'The Wheels on the Bus,' one more time, boys and girls. I know you can do it!" But her answer gives me a little pang for the year of school I missed, all because my mother said, "I'm just not ready to send Bethany out into the world all by herself yet"—as if kindergarten were full of brigands and murderers and thieves, not chunky books and brightly colored blocks and little girls in frilly socks who might have been my friends.

"It's Meadow Elementary, just a few blocks away," Myrlie is saying. "I taught . . . Oh, never mind."

I bend over my cereal and pretend to be searching for raisins. But really I'm adding up the number of times Myrlie has broken off her words in the middle of a sentence. Last night: "You just look so much like . . ." Up on the stairs: "Someone who could sleep the whole morning away like . . ." And now: "I taught . . ." I tell myself I want just one more word in one of those sentences. But it probably wouldn't be enough.

Myrlie has fallen silent again.

I take a sip of my orange juice, which is thick and full of pulp. I absolutely despise pulpy orange juice, but I swallow it anyway, as though that earns me the right to ask another question. A braver question.

"Whose room was I sleeping in?"

Myrlie frowns ruefully.

"I guess you could say it's set up for grandchildren to come and visit, but I don't have any yet. My daughter's not even married, and she says there are no prospects right now, so it'll be a while." She shrugs. "The furniture used to be my daughter's, when she was a little girl. She always wanted two beds in her room so she could have sleepovers with . . . friends."

Myrlie's words come out slower and slower as she comes to the end of her sentence, and she practically whispers the last word. A shadow crosses her face, like an echo of long-ago pain. And in that instant she looks incredibly familiar.

"You're my mother's sister, aren't you?" I blurt out. Even though she's taller, plumper, and older, Myrlie has the same straight nose, the same wide mouth, the same intense eyes as my mother. Myrlie just had to look sad for me to see the resemblance.

Her plaintive expression deepens.

"They didn't even tell you that?" she whispers.

We stare at each other, my cereal forgotten. It's as if we've just crashed through the skeletal bridge I was trying to build between us with my pitiful little questions. We're in free fall, waiting to crash into whatever lies below.

The phone rings instead.

We both jump, and Myrlie says, "I'll get it," as if there's some possibility that I'd race her for it.

She stands at the counter and offers a wary "Hello?" into the receiver. She listens, then says, "She's right here, Walter. But I'd like to talk to you too, before you hang up."

And then I am racing for the phone. I grab it from her, rudely, because I'm suddenly terrified that she'll get her conversation in first, and there won't be any time left for me.

"Daddy," I say, and Myrlie backs away. She puts away the Raisin Bran box, takes dishes to the sink. But she doesn't leave the kitchen.

"Oh, honey, it's so good to hear your voice," he says. His voice sounds tinny and artificial and far away. I feel like I can hear the distance between us over the phone.

"Where *are* you?" I say.

"I think it's better if I don't tell you that."

I can practically count on one hand the number of times my father has refused me any toy or CD or cool outfit or jewelry. But what I want now isn't a *thing*. Tears swarm in my eyes.

"Daddy . . ." I dart a glance toward Myrlie. She has her back to me; she's bent over the sink washing dishes. "Daddy, come back and get me. I can . . . I can wait with you while Mom gets help. I'll be quiet. I'll be good."

"No," he says, and his voice is like rock now. We were learning about Mohs Hardness Scale in school, right before I left home, and now I think, *Mr. Rodnow is wrong, diamond is not the hardest substance. My father's voice should be the standard.*

"I'm sorry," my father says, relenting a little. "But it's best this way. You're safe there."

Safe? I think I've been picturing my parents at some kind of psychiatric institution for very sad people. How could that not be safe? Are some of the other patients dangerous?

"Why is it safe for you if it isn't safe for me?" I ask, an edge of brattiness creeping into my voice.

"Bethany . . ." my father says helplessly, and the tears come back to my eyes. I don't want my father to be helpless. I want him to be fearless and in charge. My protector.

"I couldn't even call you last night," I complained. "I tried your cell phone, and there's something wrong, the telephone company said it was out of service. And so was my number, and Mom's, and—"

"Don't call those numbers ever again!" My father shouts. He's panicked. "In fact, just stay away from the phone unless I call. And I *will* call, as much as I can. I promise. I . . . I'll try to call once a day."

"What if I need you more often than that?" I whimper, and my vision blurs as the tears take over. The toaster I'm staring at seems to tremble before my eyes.

"Let me talk to Myrlie," my father says.

Somehow Myrlie must know that my part of the conversation is over, because she's suddenly beside me, holding out her hand for the phone.

"Why don't you go take a shower while I'm on the phone?" she says brightly, as if she can't see that I'm crying. As if I can't tell that that's just a ploy for privacy.

Numbly, I push my way out the kitchen door and trudge up the stairs. I'm nearly at the top when I hear the kitchen door latch firmly.

I stand still for a second, deciding. In my mind, I can see the cord tethering the phone into the wall, ensuring that Myrlie can't roam while she talks. Silently, I tiptoe back down the stairs and press my ear against the kitchen door.

—FIVE—

"She needs to know about Elizabeth," Myrlie is saying, ever so faintly, on the other side of the door.

She's quiet for a long time, and I worry that I'm missing huge chunks of conversation. Or that that was the end of the conversation, and she's about to come scurrying out of the kitchen, slamming the door into my ear.

"Well, of course it would be best if you and Hilary told her yourselves, but you're not here right now, are you?" Myrlie explodes.

I revise my opinion of her as the gentle, grandmotherly kindergarten teacher. I bet the kids in her class don't get away with *anything.*

There's silence again, but I know it's just because my father's talking. I've got no hope of hearing his side of this conversation.

"I'm sorry. I do understand that this must be tremendously

difficult for the two of you," Myrlie says. "But I have to be so careful about what I say around Bethany. . . . If you remember, I never was very good at keeping secrets. Or lying."

Another silence, longer this time. I study the warp of the hardwood floor beneath my feet.

"Yeah, well, I haven't had thirteen years of practice, have I?" Myrlie says. "Look, I'm happy to have Bethany stay here as long as she needs to. But she's not just some trinket you can stow away on a shelf until it's convenient for you to come back."

I'm still trying to imagine my father's response to that when Myrlie says, "Okay, we'll talk again tomorrow."

I spring back from the door and scramble up the stairs and into the bathroom. I turn on the water in the shower full blast. I peer into the mirror over the sink.

"Who is Elizabeth?" I mutter.

But the mirror offers me no reply except my own flushed, guilty reflection. And then the steam from the shower thickens, and obscures even that.

—SIX—

Myrlie is waiting for me in the living room when I creep down the stairs again, my hair wet, my face only slightly less flushed. She's holding a newspaper, but she lays it down on the couch when she hears me coming.

"I was just checking to see what's going on around town today," she says. "Something you might want to do."

I sit down on the edge of the couch and glance down at the paper. Its masthead reads THE SANDERFIELD REPORTER, with the words THE BEST SOURCE OF NEWS IN SANDERFIELD, ILLINOIS in smaller type below. It's amazing how relieved I feel, that I won't have to ask like some amnesia victim in a soap opera, "Where am I?" I'm in Sanderfield, Illinois. Not Indiana. Not Iowa. Illinois.

One small mystery solved, who knows how many huge mysteries still gaping in front of me.

"I didn't know if there were any movies you wanted to see . . . ," Myrlie says.

She lets her voice trail off, leaving an opening for my answer. I could say, "I don't care about movies. I want you to tell me who Elizabeth is." I could say, "I want you to explain why my parents are acting so weird." But I open my mouth and I can't make those words come out.

Maybe I don't quite want to know?

You're safe there, my father said over the phone. What did he mean? Am I safer being ignorant? What is he trying to keep me safe *from?*

Myrlie is watching me. She seems to have worked up to being able to stare directly at me. I imagine us spending the entire day this way: her studying me, me tongue-tied and terrified.

"Is there anywhere around here to swim?" I ask.

Myrlie does a double take.

"You like swimming?" she asks incredulously, as if I've announced that I want to go skydiving or bungee-jumping.

"I'm on a swim team," I say. "If I get out of practice, it could ruin my times for the entire season."

Coach Dinkle would be proud of my dedication, but it's not really my times I'm worried about. I just need to be in water right now. I've never tried to explain this feeling to anybody, not even the other kids on my swim team, who tend to be as obsessed about times and personal bests as Coach Dinkle is. But it's different for me.

I can remember the first time my parents took me to a swimming pool. I was three years old. Mom and Dad stood in the shallow end with me, their legs forming a protective circle around me so none of the other little kids would splash me. But something happened—maybe I slipped, maybe a little wave made it past the barrier of their bodies and knocked me down. Anyhow, my face slid under. Strangely, I wasn't scared. I didn't try to gulp in air—maybe I'd just taken a big breath already, by chance. So I opened my eyes wide and calmly looked around. The underwater world delighted me: the refraction of sunlight in the water currents, the crispness of the colors, the distortion of sound, the way every movement seemed to be in slow motion. I felt like I'd discovered a new universe, the one where I truly belonged.

My father plucked me out of the water and immediately began trying to soothe me: "There, there, Daddy won't let that bad old water get you. You're okay—"

I pushed him away.

"Again! Again!" I cried, trying to dive down out of his arms.

Mom and Dad stared at me in astonishment, sort of the same way Myrlie was staring at me now. I began howling, and nothing would satisfy me until they let me plunge back down into the water. That time I did choke a little on the water, but I didn't care. I surfaced again only long enough to get air.

"What if she drowns?" I remember Mom asking in a quavery voice.

"I guess we'll just have to teach her about holding her breath," Dad said, his voice cracking with amazement.

All the way home from the pool that day, I chanted in a singsongy voice, "I'm a mermaid, I'm a mermaid, I'm a mermaid. . . ."

I remember this mostly because of the way my parents sat so silently in the front seat of the car. They didn't keep turning around to smile at me, the way they usually did when I sang in the backseat.

Had they *wanted* me to be scared of the water?

It probably didn't help that I kept nagging them to go back to the pool after that—nagged and begged and pleaded until I was signed up for my first swimming lesson, only a week or so later.

Even if they hadn't wanted me to swim, they hadn't been able to refuse me.

From Myrlie's expression now, though, I'm kind of expecting her to tell me no.

"You'd need an indoor pool, this time of year," she says doubtfully. "I guess there's one at the Y, but I'm not a member. Let me check their guest policies."

She stands up and heads for the phone in the kitchen. I follow her because I don't know what else to do.

"This is Myrlie Wilker," she says after looking up the number and dialing. "I have a . . . uh . . . visitor staying with me who would like to go swimming. Is there any way . . . ?"

I've been studying the stenciled border that runs around the top of the kitchen walls—one painstakingly painted basket of pink and yellow and purple flowers after another. But I look at Myrlie when she says that one word: "visitor."

Why didn't she say "niece"? I wonder, and maybe the question shows up in my eyes because Myrlie's gaze darts nervously away.

"You would do that for me?" she says into the phone. "Well, thanks. We'll be there in a little bit." She hangs up and asks me, "I guess it's possible, after all. You have a swimsuit with you?"

"Sure," I say.

"You don't mind swimming after you just finished taking a shower?"

I shrug. "I don't feel like myself if I *don't* smell like chlorine," I say.

Myrlie laughs, but she has an odd expression on her face. What's so baffling about a twelve-year-old girl's wanting to swim?

Ten minutes later, we're sitting in Myrlie's car, backing out of her driveway. My seven-inch growth spurt in the past year brought me to the grand height of five feet five, which I think is supposed to be about average for an adult woman. But it's too much for Myrlie's car. My knees are practically in my ears.

"Sorry," Myrlie mutters, seeing me squirm. "This is one of the earlier gas-electric cars, and they hadn't quite worked out the size issues back then."

I look over and see that Myrlie's knees fit in perfectly under the doll-sized steering wheel. I hadn't really noticed before how much I tower over Myrlie. It's strange, since I was the shortest kid in my class from first grade through sixth grade, but I always kind of felt like I was destined to be tall. I don't dwell on it as much as I could.

"Usually it's just me driving around by myself," Myrlie is saying, still sounding apologetic. "That's why Joss talked me into buying this."

"Joss?" I say.

"My daughter." Myrlie swings her head around, checking for cars as she turns into the street. "Oh, wait, let's go the other way so you can see downtown. I'll give you the minitour of town—it won't take long."

She turns down an alley and I feel like she's changed the subject on purpose. I don't want a tour of Sanderfield; I want a roadmap of forbidden topics. Elizabeth. Joss. My parents' current location. Their reason for leaving me with Myrlie. Their reason for never mentioning her to me before last night. Her reason for not calling me her niece over the phone.

I'm just not sure if I want that roadmap so I can avoid those topics or so I can explore them.

"Abraham Lincoln once spent the night in that house over there, but it was just because his carriage wheel broke on the outskirts of town," Myrlie's saying.

She babbles a little more about historic houses and Civil War troop movements, and then we're in the town square my parents and I drove through last night, when I thought the whole place was hibernating. It doesn't look much livelier this morning, though now the lights are on in the shops: a furniture store, a florist, a Dollar General, and something called Prairie Expressions.

"Our downtown has had quite a revitalization in the past few years," Myrlie says, sounding proud. "It had kind of gone downhill there for a while—we were all really worried about our little town."

We pass the flaking-away billboard that I noticed last night, and a man is standing on a ladder beside it, peeling off its layers of years-old advertisements.

"Wonderful!" Myrlie says. "I'm so glad they're finally taking care of that eyesore. We'll be in great shape, now."

My parents and I have moved around a lot, but we've always lived in suburbs of some East Coast city. I'm used to gleaming new malls, fancy restaurants, beautifully landscaped parks. By those standards, Sanderfield—with or without the billboard— looks rundown and pathetic and forgotten. But there's something I envy in Myrlie's voice: the pride, the way she says "we."

I've never lived anywhere that inspired that tone in anyone's voice. The only "we" my family's ever been part of, really, is the three of us.

"I helped plant those flowers on the courthouse lawn," Myrlie says, pointing. "The chrysanthemums, see?"

I look, and the chrysanthemums are glorious splashes of yellow and orange, bursting across the lawn in arcs from a stone marker.

"Is there some kind of plaque over there?" I ask, squinting at a square of bronze on the marker. "What, do they engrave your name in bronze every time you plant a couple flowers?"

It's a stupid crack, but I'm surprised when Myrlie doesn't answer right away.

I glance over, and she's frozen, her fingers clenched on the steering wheel, her gaze fixed straight ahead. Then she winces, and that breaks the spell.

"No, that's . . . a memorial," she says slowly. "A memorial for someone who died a long time ago."

I can hear the effort she's making to sound nonchalant, to pass off the plaque as just another dusty historical marker that doesn't matter to anyone anymore. But she's not a very good actress.

"Who?" I want to ask. "Who's it a memorial to? Who died a long time ago?"

For a moment I think I actually have asked those questions aloud, because Myrlie glances at me quickly, her face a troubled mask. Then she goes back to staring at the street ahead, as if she's wearing blinders.

And then it's too late for me to ask anything, too awkward. We drive the rest of the way in silence.

The Y is a low, sprawling building, surprisingly large for a town the size of Sanderfield. We stop at the front desk, and a cheerful-faced woman greets Myrlie.

"You were in a hurry to get here! I'll fill out all the paper-work so you can go right in. I'll just need your name . . ."

She's looking at me, so I say, "Bethany. Bethany Cole. C-o-l-e."

Out of the corner of my eye, I see Myrlie's head jerk back and her eyebrows squint together. It's like she's surprised to hear my last name, like she didn't know what it was or she thought it was something different. But when I turn and look at her directly, she's managed to iron out her expression.

The woman at the desk has her head bent over the papers. She sees nothing.

"Address?" she says.

"It's thirty-eight, fifty-two Tyler Av—" I start to reel out my Greenleaf, Pennsylvania, address, though it already seems nearly as far away and long ago as all the other houses my parents and I left behind.

Myrlie interrupts.

"Oh, just put down the same address as mine," she says. "Six-oh-five Morning Street. It's probably easier to have every-thing local, isn't it?"

"Um, I guess," the woman says doubtfully.

"And are you sure I can't pay something?" Myrlie asks. "I'm perfectly willing—"

The woman waves away the offer, the cheerful grin restored to her face.

"Oh, no, Mrs. Wilker. After what you did for my little

Ronald, believe me, this is the least I can do. I tell everyone I wasn't sure he was even human until we moved here and I sent him off to kindergarten, and you turned him around. I'll just put you down as my guest, and Bethany down as Ronald's, and there's no charge."

She beams at Myrlie and Myrlie thanks her, and we head for the locker room.

I already put my bathing suit on under my clothes, so all I have to do is yank off my jeans and sweater, and toss them and my glasses and bag into a locker. After those few strange, awkward moments in the car and at the desk, I'm even more eager to immerse myself in chlorinated water, to think of nothing for the next hour but the pull of my strokes, the power of my kicks. There's a kind of etiquette of locker rooms, anyhow, that even if you yourself haven't stripped down to total nudity, you don't look around too much in case someone else has. So I'm not paying attention to anything except the need to grab my goggles and towel, to shut my locker door.

That makes it all the more jarring when I turn and come face to face with a strange woman who's absolutely staring at me, her jaw agape, her eyes practically popping out of their sockets.

"It can't be . . . ," she murmurs.

Behind her a little girl who's maybe three or four shivers in a wet towel.

"*Mommy,*" she complains. "I'm cold. Aren't you going to help me get changed?"

The woman doesn't seem to hear, she's so transfixed staring at me. The woman actually lifts her hand and brushes her fingers against my skin, as if to prove to herself that I'm not a hallucination.

"I . . . ," she says, and seems to recover control of herself a little bit. "I'm sorry. You just look so much like someone I used to know. Years ago. When I was your age, and not middle-aged and loopy and . . ." She gestures toward her stomach. Squinting, I realize that her stomach sticks far out over the waistband of her workout pants. She's pregnant.

She's also still blinking like she can't believe her eyes.

"This is just amazing," she says. "Are you by any chance related to—?"

"She's related to me." It's Myrlie, coming up behind me from the bathroom on the other side of the locker room.

The woman takes a step back, practically stepping on her daughter's toes.

"Oh. That makes sense, then, I guess," she says. But she still sounds dazed, she's still staring at me.

"How have you been doing lately, Tammy?" Myrlie asks. "How's Bryce adjusting to second grade?"

"Oh, um, fine," the woman says vaguely. She tears her gaze away from me. "Why aren't you at school today, Mrs. Wilker? You aren't sick, are you?"

"No, no," Myrlie says. "I just took a personal day. First one in more than twenty years. It's kind of refreshing to see what the rest of the world does between eight and three."

She smiles, and under the cover of that smile I slip out of the locker room and into the pool area. Then I'm underwater, my arms flailing, my legs threshing. But no matter how furiously I swim, I can't outpace my thoughts.

That woman's expression was straight out of a horror movie, I think, trying—and failing—to swim even faster. *If I were a director, that's just how I'd tell an actress to look.*

If she saw a ghost.

—SEVEN—

I swim until my legs are rubbery and my arms feel like so much limp spaghetti. I've had the kind of practice where, as Coach Dinkle puts it, I've left skid marks on the turn walls.

But as I haul myself out of the lap lane, I still can't convince myself that I'm wrong about the woman in the locker room. Tammy. I've tried every theory I can think of. My best two are that she's crazy, or that I just misread her expression because I didn't have my glasses on. But I'm not so nearsighted that I couldn't see someone standing right in front of me. And she seemed perfectly sane, except for the little matter of acting like she'd seen a ghost.

"Done?" Myrlie asks, handing me my towel.

I'm not sure what she's been doing for the past two hours, but she starts glancing around nervously as soon as I'm out of the water. She's right behind me as we walk into the locker room. I feel like I have an escort. Maybe this is what it's like to be the President, always surrounded by Secret Service officers.

The locker room is empty—Tammy and her little girl must have left a long time ago. But Myrlie still peers around anxiously, as if another Tammy might pop up any minute.

"I'll grab a shower and change in there," I say, because she's creeping me out. I pull my clothes from the locker. I hide behind the vinyl curtain of the shower stall and let the water stream over my body.

When I emerge, fully dressed and ready to go, I find that Myrlie has stationed herself right outside the stall. The way she's standing, I'm tempted to ask, "Is the coast clear?" But it's not a joking matter. And my last joke wasn't exactly a big success.

Myrlie hustles me out of the locker room and past the friendly woman at the front desk—Ronald's mom—who barely gets a nod. Once we're in the car, Myrlie throws the gearshift into reverse and exits the parking lot so quickly we're spitting gravel. She drives back through town, silent and grim-faced.

Then we're back in her driveway. She turns off the ignition. Neither of us makes a move to open a door and get out. We just sit there.

"Who?" I whisper, surprising myself. I clear my throat. I can make myself heard. I have to. "Who did she think I looked like?"

—EIGHT—

Myrlie's expression reminds me of those speeded-up Doppler radar views on the Weather Channel, where violent storm systems spin and collide and zoom away, all in a matter of seconds. She looks surprised and relieved and angry and defensive and sad, very sad. Then resigned.

"I can't tell you," she says. "I'm sorry. I promised your father I wouldn't talk about . . . that."

Disappointment pours over me. I muscled up the courage to ask—don't I deserve a better answer than that? A real answer?

Myrlie is still watching me.

Get out of the car, Myrlie, I think bitterly. *Walk away. That's how my parents deal with questions they don't want to answer.*

My anger surprises me, because I've never quite counted up all the unanswered questions before. I have a whole lifetime's worth.

Where did you live when you were a little girl, Mommy?

Why don't I have a grandma and a grandpa like Gretchen and Emily and Tommy and Michael do?

Why do we have to move again?

Why is everyone else's mommy and daddy younger than my mommy and daddy?

Are you mad at me?

How come everybody else in my class has a brother or a sister, and I don't?

Why are you crying, Mommy?

Where are you going, Daddy? Why are you leaving me here?

Where are you now?

Tears rush into my eyes, but I'm not going to cry. I'm not going to be like my mother, weak and sniveling and frail. I am taller than her; I outgrew her. I do not cry. I am fierce and strong and I just swam two miles.

And Myrlie is still watching me. She didn't get out of the car and walk away.

I take a deep breath, very deliberate. Steadying.

"Is it Elizabeth?" I ask. "Do I look like Elizabeth?"

Myrlie doesn't have to say yes or no, because I see the answer in her eyes, her gentle, kind, not-good-at-lying eyes.

"How did you find out about Elizabeth?" she asks.

My mind races, searching for a lie that will free Myrlie from her promise to my dad. If I pretend to know everything already, she can't get in trouble for telling. Can she?

But I'm not good at lying, either. I don't have any practice. My parents were always right there, watching me, so I never got a chance to make up alternate versions of my life that any-one would believe.

"I don't know about Elizabeth," I admit. "I just heard the name. But . . . can't you tell me now?"

Myrlie looks heavenward, or at least toward the ceiling of her car. Then she looks back at me.

"Bethany," she says gently, "you have to understand. I'm a teacher. I've spent my life taking care of other people's children—shaping them and molding them and trying to do my best to have them turn out right. After all these years, I've come to accept that there are limits to what I can do for somebody else's child. Even when it breaks my heart. Even when I think the parents are wrong."

"*You* think I should know," I choke out.

"I do," Myrlie agrees. "But I won't tell you."

I'm shaking my head, angrier than ever.

"That's not fair!" I complain.

Myrlie takes her hand off the steering wheel and lays it over mine.

"Don't think too badly of your parents," Myrlie says, still in that infuriatingly calm voice. "They're doing what *they* believe is best for you. And I have to say, I only raised one child of my own, but it was no easier supposedly having all the power, all the control."

I'm one step away from rolling my eyes—"morphing into a teenager," as my friend Lucy calls it. She has three older brothers and sisters, and she had years of observing their obnoxious teenaged behavior. She claims to have done her first successful eye roll at age five. She's a master at it.

Here I am, almost thirteen, and I've never gotten a chance to perfect my technique. It's hard to roll your eyes at someone who's sobbing.

"If . . ." Myrlie begins, then breaks off, listening.

The phone is ringing inside her house.

Both of us spring out of the car, bound up the stairs to the back door. It leads into a covered back porch, and then there's another door into the kitchen. Myrlie fumbles with keys; I jerk on the doorknob even though I know the door is locked.

Finally the door is open and we both spill in, then zoom across the kitchen floor. I reach the phone first.

"Hello?" I shout into the receiver. "Daddy?"

I hear a click, then a dial tone.

"Hello?" I say again. "Hello?"

"No one's there," Myrlie says, gently.

"He hung up. He didn't wait. . . ." And even though I am fierce and strong and just swam two miles, I feel myself sinking toward despair. I slide down toward the floor.

Myrlie catches me.

"It might not have even been him," she says. "If it was, he'll call again."

"Don't you have caller I.D.?" I ask. "Or can't we do 'dial-back'? It's 'star' something, I think, sixty-nine or sixty-seven or . . ."

I'm reaching back up toward the phone, maybe reaching for a phone book to look up the right number. But Myrlie's shaking her head.

"No," she says apologetically. "My phone company charges extra fees for fancy stuff like that, and I never had either of those services installed. I've just never needed anything like that before. But don't worry. He'll call back."

I drop my arm, and Myrlie hugs me tighter.

I picture the two of us in a movie scene, a grandmotherly

type and a preteen girl clutching each other, slumped on the linoleum floor of an old-fashioned kitchen, the phone cord dangling above us. The scene is too stark for the kind of movies I'm used to seeing. Hollywood would have to add a sarcastic voice-over to lighten the mood, something like, "And then I learned that if you have to be abandoned by your parents in a thicket of mysteries, it's not so bad to be left with someone like Myrlie, who's used to comforting five-year-olds for a living. Just try to pick a Myrlie who also believes in caller I.D."

In real life, I'm too far gone to appreciate sarcasm. All I can do is clutch Myrlie and try not to cry.

—NINE—

Eventually we get up off the floor and fix lunch. It's an odd transition: One minute I'm slumped over on the linoleum, lost in despair, the next, I'm standing with Myrlie in front of a cabinet, examining her collection of Campbell soups.

"I'm sorry, I just don't keep much food around," she says. "I'm sure you're used to better than this—Hillary's such a great cook."

I don't tell Myrlie that my dad and I have been living on Budget Gourmet and Lean Cuisine and Stouffer's for the past few months. Freezer to microwave to table in five minutes or less. It occurs to me now, standing in front of Myrlie's cabinet, that I could have made more of an effort. Mom did teach me how to cook, back in the days before the constant sobbing. I could have at least boiled some water, thrown in some spaghetti, heated up some jarred sauce. Fed myself and my father.

You don't know what it was like, I want to protest to some-body—maybe Myrlie. *Living with all that crying, it saps your spirit. Makes you feel like you don't deserve anything better than Budget Gourmet.*

But Myrlie hasn't accused me of anything, and some form of pride stops me from saying anything bad about my parents.

In the end, we settle on tomato soup and grilled cheese sandwiches.

"Here's a pan. Why don't you heat up the soup while I make the sandwiches?" Myrlie says.

It strikes me as incredibly quaint and old-fashioned—even touching—that Myrlie expects me to cook the soup on the stovetop instead of in the microwave.

"I can go to the grocery this afternoon," Myrlie says as she slices cheese. "I'll lay in some supplies, in case you're here for a while."

How long? I want to ask. *What's 'a while' mean?* But maybe Myrlie promised my dad not to tell me that either. And I'm worn out; it's easier to keep our conversation on the level of tomato soup versus chicken with stars, and "Do you like lots of cheese on your sandwiches or just a thin layer?"

Then I look over, and Myrlie's biting her lip. Grimacing.

"I remember, my daughter always hated going to the gro-cery store with me, once she got to be your age," Myrlie says in a too-loud, too-careful, artificial voice. "You can stay here while I go. I could download some movies on the TV for you, if you like."

I stir milk into the soup and watch the whirls of white turn red. I don't think Myrlie is really worried about my hating gro-cery shopping.

She's scared we'll run into another Tammy. She doesn't want me to be recognized again.

But suspecting that—knowing that?—doesn't do me any good. I'm not sure whether I should call Myrlie's bluff or whether I should just play along. I've got no compass for navigating this situation.

But it's cozy in the kitchen, stirring soup, smelling grilled bread. It seems so normal. I crave normalcy, even if it's just a facade.

"All right," I say.

So Myrlie has me help her make a grocery list after we eat. Do I like chicken? Pasta? Tacos? Stir-fry?

"Nothing with nuts, right?" she says, her pen flying across the page.

"Absolutely," I say.

"And I bet you're a big fan of blueberry muffins."

"Uh-huh."

She's already written it down. There's a half-smile on her face.

"Peaches-and-cream oatmeal?" she asks. She's not even watching for me to nod my head.

"Wait a minute. How did you know that?" Something like panic churns in my stomach.

"Oh, just a guess." Myrlie looks up now, jolted, the smile gone. "I just thought you *might* like it. Do you?"

I do. I love it. I used to eat peaches-and-cream oatmeal for breakfast all the time, until I decided Froot Loops made me seem more like a normal kid.

"No!" I say. "I hate peaches-and-cream oatmeal."

"Okay," Myrlie says, shrugging as if we're still just talking about food. "What would you like me to buy for your breakfasts?"

And I swear her bottom lip starts to curl back under her top teeth, starts to make the first sounds of "Froot Loops."

"Corn Pops!" I say, too emphatically. "They're my favorite!"

"Okay," Myrlie says, and she writes it down.

But I think she knows I'm lying.

—TEN—

Before she leaves, Myrlie shows me how the TV works and how to download movies on her cable system. She looks up the number for the grocery store and writes it down in big, fat numbers on a pad of paper beside the phone. She apologizes for being "probably the last person in America who doesn't have a cell phone." She asks me at least six times, "Now, you're sure you'll be okay by yourself? If you need me for anything—anything at all—just call the grocery store and have me paged."

"Sure," I say. "I'll be fine."

And then Myrlie's gone, and the house is dead silent. I stand at the window watching her blue car disappear from sight, and I feel abandoned once again. I stumble back and sit on the couch and I listen for a sound, any sound—the hum of the refrigerator, the tick of a clock, the breathing of the furnace. There's nothing.

This is something else strange about me, which I never would have admitted to Myrlie or anyone else, but here I am, twelve going on thirteen, and I have never once been alone. Oh, sure, sometimes I've gone to my room and shut the door, shutting my parents out. But even then I always knew they were there in the house, just the other side of a wall, within earshot. Way back in third grade I started hearing from other kids at school how they got themselves out the door in the morning, an hour or two after their parents left for work; how they went home to an empty house and popped microwave popcorn and watched TV cartoons and didn't even touch their homework until their parents straggled in the door.

By third grade I had the sense not to ask for this treat for myself. My mother would have popped microwave popcorn for me; she would have turned the TV to the right station long before I got home from school; she would have sat on the couch with me, pretending to be just as interested as I was in *Rugrats* and *SpongeBob SquarePants* and *DivaGirls*.

The wind blows outside and tree branches scratch against the house and I jump half a foot off the couch. I start thinking of those old third-grade classmates of mine as incredibly brave, not incredibly privileged.

"Stop it!" I say aloud. "You're almost thirteen years old and you're perfectly safe. Isn't that why your father left you here?" My voice sounds quavery and terrified. I reach for the TV remote, hoping for some movie I can drown my cowardice in for the next hour and a half. I hear a rustling sound, and I jump again, but it's just the newspaper Myrlie was reading earlier, the *Sanderfield Reporter*, sliding down to the ground.

"You know, there could be a whole article in there about

Elizabeth, and you wouldn't even know it because you're such a chicken," I goad myself.

I don't really believe there's anything about Elizabeth in the newspaper, but I pick it up anyway and start reading. The front page is all about the president's latest speech and some embezzler in Chicago who's getting out of prison. Further in, I have my choice of reading about a P.T.O. pancake breakfast or a street improvement project.

"Guess someone forgot to tell the *Sanderfield Reporter* that much more interesting things are happening in my life right now, right here under their noses," I say. I'm really beginning to annoy myself with this talking out loud. It's probably an early sign of mental illness.

Like Mom's? I think this, rather than saying it, but that's hardly comforting.

I turn another page of the paper, and my eyes light on a photo of a dozen women posing behind a swath of flowers. SANDERFIELD LADIES CLUB SPRUCES UP COURTHOUSE LAWN is the caption, and Myrlie's face floats fuzzily in the back row of the picture. But my eyes focus on what's behind her and the other women: the stone memorial.

For someone who died a long time ago, Myrlie had said, looking stricken, before we got to the Y, before Tammy mistook me for someone she'd known years ago, when she was my age. Before Tammy looked like she'd seen a ghost.

The way Tammy and Myrlie acted, I'm pretty sure Elizabeth is dead. And the woman at the front desk of the Y, whose little boy was born before she moved here, didn't seem to notice anything unusual about my appearance. So probably Elizabeth died a long time ago.

What if Elizabeth was the person memorialized on the plaque? What if the plaque had her full name on it, first and last? If I just got a glimpse of that plaque, maybe the birth and death dates for good measure, I could use Myrlie's computer—surely she has a computer—crank up a search engine, and find out everything I want to know. I wouldn't need Myrlie to break her promise. I wouldn't need my dad to decide it was safe to tell me the truth.

I'd just need to walk to the courthouse by myself. Now, before Myrlie comes back.

I don't move.

It's not really that I'm scared. What's there to be frightened of, walking a few blocks in tiny Sanderfield, Illinois, in broad daylight on a crisp October afternoon?

"I don't know," I mutter, and that's the problem. I feel like I'm trying to put a thousand-piece jigsaw puzzle together with all but two or three of the pieces turned upside down. Maybe there is something to be afraid of, if Dad said I'd be "safe" at Myrlie's house. Will I still be safe four or five blocks away?

From the time I was a little girl, I've hated sitting still, doing nothing. It's that, finally, that propels me off the couch.

"I just decided to take a walk, get some air," I say, practicing excuses in case Myrlie comes home and catches me gone. I even write her a note on the tablet by the phone, under the grocery store's number: "Be right back. B." After all, it's not like she told me I couldn't go anywhere.

My heart's pounding like I'm doing something horribly forbidden, but I try to ignore it.

I also pretend to myself that it's perfectly normal to zip my windbreaker up to the very top, to pull up my hood so it covers my hair and most of my face. I step outside, latching the door behind me but not locking it, and this, too, I try to defend. *People leave their doors unlocked all the time in small towns, don't they?* A stiff breeze hits me in the face and I tell myself it's bracing, steadying. I take deep breaths and make it to the end of the block.

Nobody's out walking except me, and I feel horribly visible to all the cars driving by. I hunch over, keep my head down. I turn right, then left, wait at a traffic light, and go straight. And somehow, fighting fear and panic and a slight sense that what I'm doing is ridiculous, I reach the courthouse square.

My legs start shaking as I climb two concrete steps toward the memorial. The writing on the plaque is in fancy script that's not easy to read, but even with all the frills and flourishes, even from six feet away, I can tell: The first name's not long enough.

It's "Thomas," not "Elizabeth."

Brilliant work, Nancy Drew, I think in disgust. *You're so egotistical. Why would a plaque on a stone in Sanderfield, Illinois, have anything to do with you?*

I read the rest of the plaque anyhow.

IN MEMORY OF

THOMAS WILKER

A GOOD MAN AND A GREAT MAYOR

1949–1991

Wilker, I think. *Thomas Wilker. Myrlie Wilker. Is this her father? Grandfather?*

I remember that "Wilker" is probably Myrlie's married

name. People at the Y called her "Mrs." I do the math. This Thomas Wilker was forty-two when he died, some twenty years ago. Myrlie is probably in her late fifties or early sixties. She and Thomas would have been about the same age.

I've got no proof, but I'm certain: This plaque is a memorial to Myrlie's husband.

—ELEVEN—

I walk back to Myrlie's house, leaves crunching under my feet. I feel like I'm stepping on carcasses.

It's too much, I think. *Mom crying and Dad being worried and me looking like some girl who's probably dead and no one telling me anything, and Myrlie's husband dying.* . . . I know it's strange to act like Myrlie's newly widowed, but that's how I feel, because I just found out about it.

I pass the house that Myrlie said Abraham Lincoln slept in once, and somehow that seems unbearably sad too. When he was in Sanderfield, Lincoln didn't know he was going to be assassinated, he didn't know almost all the young men in town were going to go off and die in the war, he didn't even know there was going to be a war. . . .

I'm doing what I used to do when I was a little girl and Mom would start crying. Spiraling down. We'd be sitting on the couch and Mom would be reading one of my favorite books to me—*Mrs. Piggle-Wiggle,* maybe, or *Madeline* or *Pippi Long-stocking*—and Mom's voice would start sounding thick. I'd look up and Mom would have tears streaming down her face. And I'd feel those tears tugging at me. Pretty soon I'd be crying too. And Mom would start comforting *me*: "There, there, everything's all right. You've got Mommy. I've got you."

I think maybe that's why the home-schooling ended, because my father came home from work and found the two of us crying on the couch together.

But I don't know why Mom cried only every once in a while then, and cries all the time now. I don't know when I learned how to separate, so I could watch Mom crying her heart out and feel absolutely positively nothing.

I wish I could separate myself from my sadness now. Why should I care that Myrlie's husband died twenty years ago? Why should I feel anything for Myrlie, whom I didn't even meet until yesterday?

Because she's nice, I think. *Because she cares about me. Because she's all I've got right now.*

I let myself in the front door at Myrlie's house and tear up the note I left for her. Then I plop down in front of the TV and try to lose myself in some stupid movie about jewel thieves making one last heist. That's what I'm watching when Myrlie gets home.

"Hi," I grunt. I know I could jump up and offer to help her carry in the groceries. I could ask her about her husband—as far as I know, *he's* not a forbidden topic. But I don't do either of those things. I just stare at unrealistic car chases flickering before my eyes.

Somehow Myrlie and I get through the rest of the day. I

watch TV; she cooks up a sumptuous dinner of chicken and stuffing and peas and those little baby onions that I love but I'm pretty sure I didn't mention to Myrlie. It doesn't matter. I can't make myself choke down more than a bite or two of anything.

"I'm really tired. I think I'll just go to bed now," I tell Myrlie.

Myrlie glances at the pile of dishes in the sink, but all she says is, "Okay."

I climb the stairs alone. After I've brushed my teeth and turned out the light and crawled into bed, I lay in the darkness telling myself, "Daddy will call in the morning. He will. He'll call you. Daddy will call in the morning." As mantras go, it's not terribly comforting. And, as it turns out, it's not exactly accurate. Dad doesn't call me.

Mom does.

—TWELVE—

The phone rings in the middle of the night. I'm
running to answer it before I quite remember where I am. I
crash into the wall trying to find the door; I trip on the bottom
two stairsteps. Still, I reach the kitchen long before Myrlie.

"Hello?" I gasp, out of breath.

"Elizabeth?" It's my mother's voice, but my mother's voice
with a difference: She's not crying. "Elizabeth, I am so glad I
reached you. I know you're spending the night with Joss, but I
just had the worst dream, and I wanted to make sure—"

"Mom, this is Bethany," I say.

Mom actually laughs.

"Oh, is that the name you're trying out this week? Enough,
already. Listen, Elizabeth, I know you were counting on going
to Sinclair Mountain for your birthday, but I don't think it's a
good idea. This dream I had . . . Well, let's just say it'd be better if
you stayed home. We could rent some videos, have a party—"

"Mom, it's *Bethany*," I say. I have chills traveling up my spine.

"Quit fooling around, Elizabeth. I'm serious. I know you're disappointed about Sinclair Mountain, but, believe me, this is for the best—"

In the background, I hear a kind of grunt, and my father saying, drowsily, "Hillary! Who are you talking to?"

"Elizabeth," my mom says. Her next words are muffled, as if she's put her hand over the phone: "I just had to call her. I had this horrible dream about her birthday at Sinclair Mountain. And it was all so real—"

I hear a clunking sound, as if the phone has fallen to the floor, then my father's voice, louder than before. He's talking directly into the receiver now.

"Hello?"

"Daddy?" I say.

"Bethany?" Even he sounds a little uncertain about my identity.

"Daddy, what's going on? What's Mom talking about? Who's Elizabeth? Why doesn't Mom know who I am?"

I can hear my father taking a ragged breath as my mother shouts in the background, "Walter, give me that phone! I have to talk to her! I don't want her to die . . ." The "die" fades away into a wail and then sobs.

"Daddy?" I say again.

"Hillary, *stop!* You're upsetting Bethany. Remember Bethany?" My father's voice is a distant rumble. Then he's back on the phone. "Your mother had a bad reaction to some medication. That's all. She's . . . hallucinating."

"No, she's not," I say. I'm not sure my father can hear me

over my mother's sobbing, and somehow this emboldens me. "Elizabeth was real, wasn't she? And I look like her. Who was she? *Did* she die?"

For a moment, all I can hear is my mother's sobbing. Then my father whispers into the phone, "Yes."

"Yes, what?" I say. "Yes, she's real? Yes, she's dead? Yes, I look like her?"

"We didn't think we'd have to tell you," my father says. His voice is still barely more than a whisper. I press the phone so tightly against my ear that I can hear my own pulse echoing against the receiver. And behind my pulse, the rest of his words: "We didn't want you to be upset."

"Upset?" I repeat. "Didn't you think I'd be upset wondering why Mom cries all the time? Didn't you think I'd be upset getting dropped off with some relative I've never even heard of, while you and Mom are God knows where?"

One of my teachers back in Pennsylvania, Mr. Kaffi, always quoted at us, "You shall know the truth, and the truth shall set you free." It's from the Bible or somewhere. I don't know anything resembling the truth about Elizabeth yet, but it sure feels wonderful to *speak* the truth. It's liberating. Suddenly, I love shouting at my father.

"Yes . . . I don't know," my father says, and he sounds so old and defeated, I stop feeling so wonderful. "Ask . . . ask Myrlie. Myrlie can tell you about Elizabeth."

"She's allowed to?" I feel cruel pressing this point, like a lawyer badgering a distraught witness on the stand. But I've come so far, I don't want permission snatched away from me at the last minute. I can picture Myrlie shaking her head at me, saying, "Well, maybe your father told *you* I was allowed to tell, but he didn't tell *me.*" It'd be like the little-kid game, losing at the very end because you didn't say, "Mother, may I?"

My father sighs, a heavy, pained, I'm-not-sure-I-can-survive-this sigh.

"Let me talk to Myrlie," he says.

I look around and she's right there, leaning against the counter in her red fuzzy robe, her white hair tousled, her face creased with concern. I don't know how long she's been there or how much she's heard, but I hand her the phone.

"Walter?" she says, and listens. And listens. Finally she says, "I can do that. Take care of Hillary," and hangs up.

The phone's in its cradle and Myrlie turns to face me. My heart pounds hard against my chest, as though I just swam the hardest practice of my life. What have I gotten myself into? I dread the words that Myrlie is about to say. She opens her mouth. She speaks. I hear her voice as if I'm drowning and she's far away on shore.

"Elizabeth," she says, "was your sister."

I pull back. I'm drowning for sure.

"I'm an only child," I say.

Myrlie puts her hand on top of mine, on top of the counter. Holding on to me.

"So was Elizabeth," she says.

—THIRTEEN—

I stare at Myrlie in confusion, as if she's just told me one of those impossible-sounding brainteasers, like if a plane crashes on the border of Mexico and the United States, where are all the survivors buried? (Answer: Nowhere. The survivors are still alive.) How could Elizabeth and I be sisters if both of us are only children?

Oh.

"Only one survivor," I mutter, which probably makes Myrlie think I've lost my mind. "You mean, Elizabeth died before I was born."

"Yes," Myrlie says, and for a minute, I think that's all she's going to tell me. But then she gestures toward the kitchen table and says, "Sit down."

We sit in opposing chairs, and although Myrlie doesn't begin her story, "Once upon a time," I still feel like I'm hearing a tale about a long-ago time that's not quite real.

"Hillary and I grew up in this house," Myrlie says. "Hillary married Walter and I married Tom and we moved into houses just around the corner from here. And then we each had one daughter. Elizabeth came first, in June of 1978, then Jocelyn— my Joss—was born that August."

I try to figure out how long ago 1978 was, but my mind's not capable of math right now. It seems like an eternity ago, another lifetime.

It was another lifetime, I think. Elizabeth's lifetime.

Myrlie's smiling, a misty, far-away look in her eye.

"Elizabeth and Joss were so tight, more like sisters than cousins. The very best of friends. They were always together. And Hillary and I became closer, because of them."

I picture two little girls toddling around, falling over one another like puppies at play. I'm not sure what Joss should look like, but I give Elizabeth my blond hair, my hazel eyes. And then, somehow, I'm jealous. Elizabeth had my parents and my hair and my eyes *and* best friend/almost-sister/cousin Joss. At that age, I had Gretchen Dunlap across the street telling me I was a spoiled brat.

Myrlie's still smiling.

"The summer Joss and Elizabeth both turned six, they fell in love with the Olympics. Do you know who Mary Lou Retton is? The gymnast? She won five medals in 'eighty-four. She was the star, and all Joss and Elizabeth wanted was to *be* Mary Lou. You should have seen all the cartwheels they did, the somersaults. . . . Off the couches, across the yard, down the stairs . . . Hillary and I signed them up for gymnastics lessons mostly because we thought the girls would end up killing themselves otherwise. We figured there would be mats at the gymnastics lessons, mats and spotters and safe techniques. . . ."

"And were there?" I ask. I'm bracing myself for the end of this happy story, when I know Elizabeth is going to die.

"Of course," Myrlie says. Her fingers fidget with the edge of the placemat in front of her. "I know you're going to think I'm just a proud mother, a proud aunt, but Joss and Elizabeth were good at gymnastics. Really good. Naturals, people said. Pretty soon we were driving them an hour away, a couple times a week, because there were better gymnastics teachers in Ridgetown. It . . . changed the way they were raised, them being gymnasts."

"That makes sense," I say, though I'm wondering, *Did swimming change anything about how I was raised?*

"You have to understand," Myrlie says. "We had people telling us they were going to be the medal hopes for the 'ninety-two Olympics."

"They went to the Olympics?" In spite of myself, I'm impressed.

Myrlie shakes her head.

"We didn't make it to 'ninety-two," she says sadly, and at first I think that's ridiculous. Myrlie's in her fifties or sixties now—obviously she lived through 1992. Then I realize: *She means Elizabeth. Elizabeth didn't make it to '92.*

"It was Elizabeth's thirteenth birthday," Myrlie says. Her voice has taken on a hypnotic quality, as if she *has* to tell this story now. And I have to listen. "June 13, 1991. A beautiful day. We took the girls to Sinclair Mountain to celebrate."

"Sinclair Mountain?" I say numbly. In my head, I'm replaying my mother's voice on the phone: *I had this horrible dream about her birthday at Sinclair Mountain. . . .*

"It's a big amusement park, west of here," Myrlie says. "With rides and games and roller coasters—oh, how those girls loved the roller coasters! It was just the six of us who went, the two families. Walter and Thomas took the day off work. But we kept joking about how the girls didn't really need us, they just checked in when they ran out of money. It was the first time we let them run around on their own like that."

Myrlie falls silent. I feel such a growing sense of dread that I prompt her: "And . . . ?"

"There was an accident when we were driving home. Thomas and Elizabeth were killed." She says the words flat out, without emotion. She blinks, as if surprised that she's come to the end of the story so quickly.

I'm struggling to figure out what I feel. I was overwhelmed with sadness this afternoon looking at the memorial for Myrlie's husband, even though I knew nothing about him. Elizabeth was my *sister*, my long-lost sister, almost exactly my same age when she died, a promising athlete cut down in her prime. And I feel nothing.

It just doesn't seem real.

"So . . ." I say slowly. "My parents were really sad for a long time, I bet. But eventually they had me and that probably helped, didn't it? Cheered them up?"

I want so badly to turn this story around, to end on a happy note—with my birth, not Elizabeth's death.

Myrlie winces, and I think I've probably been insensitive, not saying anything about her husband.

"I suppose," she says slowly. "I only saw Hillary and Walter a few times after that. At the funerals. And then they left town. . . . It was too hard, I think, for them to stay here."

"You stayed," I say, fiercely.

"Well . . . ," Myrlie says. "I was away a lot at first, because Joss was hurt pretty badly in the accident, and she was in the hospital up in Chicago for a long time. I was there at her bedside pretty much around the clock. And then when she got out of the hospital, I didn't think I had any choice but to come back here. I know it's probably hard for you to understand, how we could go from being so close, to me not even knowing where Hillary and Walter lived. To them not even telling me when you were born. It's just, we were all so . . . shattered by the accident. I think sometimes tragedies bring people together, and sometimes they pull them apart. And that's what happened to us. The grief came between us."

"Didn't Mom and Dad visit Joss in the hospital?" I ask, because I want to believe that my parents did something besides just showing up twenty years later to dump their new daughter out on Myrlie's doorstep.

But Myrlie shakes her head.

"I don't really blame them," she says, as if she's read my mind. "I did then—and that made things worse. But I think it was too hard on them to see that I still had a daughter, when theirs was dead. It was hard on me to see Hillary with Walter, when my husband was dead."

We've circled back to death again. Myrlie's fiddling with the placemat once more.

"I am not unhappy now," she says carefully, patting the placemat back into place. "I have a good life—lots of friends, a fulfilling job. A daughter. I miss Tom, but I'm not sad anymore. The hole in my life has been not knowing about Hillary and Walter."

I feel like Myrlie's trying to tell me something beyond the simple meaning of her words.

"Did you ever try to find them?" I ask.

"I thought they didn't want to be found. They knew where I was. I've had the same phone number since 1977."

I think about all the times my parents and I have moved: when I was one, when I was two, when I was six and nine and eleven. Were we moving so Myrlie couldn't track us down? But then why would Dad drive back here and leave me—just me—with Myrlie?

"There's something else I should tell you . . . ," Myrlie says hesitantly. "Something that might help you understand. That night when we were coming back from Sinclair Mountain . . . your mother was driving. She thought the accident was her fault."

"Was it?" I ask. I think about how my mother drives on the rare occasions she gets behind the wheel of our car: hunched over, with a pinched look on her face. Now that I think about it, I don't believe she's driven even once since school was out last June.

June.

"Was it her fault?" I ask again.

Myrlie gestures helplessly.

"Nobody knows," she says. "Nobody will ever know."

—FOURTEEN—

It's nearly five in the morning when I crawl back into my bed, feeling like a totally different person than when I left it.

"Sleep as late as you want," Myrlie says from the doorway. "I won't wake you."

She turns out the light and shuts the door, but I don't fall asleep. I'm replaying every word she said, recasting everything I thought I knew. Every single one of my memories seems different now. I've spent my entire life with a ghost haunting my family, and I didn't even know it. Or did I?

"I'm the bestest girl ever, aren't I?" I remember asking my mother one afternoon when I was four or five, when I'd finished what I thought was a particularly beautiful finger painting.

"Of course," Mom said. But the next time I looked up from my finger paints, she was gone. I tiptoed around the corner and found her sprawled across her bed, sobbing into her pillow.

"Are you okay, Mommy?" I asked.

"Oh, yes," she sniffed. "I just got something in my eye."

Or maybe that wasn't the excuse she used—maybe it was "My allergies are acting up again," or "This cold makes my eyes water," or "This always happens when I'm chopping onions." She's used all sorts of different explanations over the years.

But I think that must have been the first time I didn't believe her. I remember standing there watching her pretend she wasn't crying, and inside me a little voice was whispering, *You're not the bestest.* I accidentally left a little smudge of black finger paint on the wall that afternoon, and as long as we lived in that house, looking at that smudge could make me feel bad. Anytime I sat at the kitchen table after that, I had to keep my back to the smudge, and even then I knew it was there.

And now I understand.

I couldn't be Mom's "bestest girl ever" because Elizabeth had been that first, I think.

I remember another time, when my father caught me riding my bicycle without a helmet. My parents did everything but provide airbags when I used a trike or a bike or a scooter; I had kneepads and elbow pads and wrist guards and even special gloves that gave me extra grip. One of the neighborhood dads used to think it was funny to ask if my parents were suiting me up for the NFL. Maybe that's why I decided to break the rules that particular day; maybe I just liked to feel the wind streaming through my hair, free and unencumbered. But when my father found me, he yanked me off the bike, his hands shaking, his voice trembling as he yelled, "Don't you know you could be killed?"

And I laughed.

"No, Daddy. *Kids* don't die. Just old people."

He jerked back, like I'd slapped him.

"Oh, honey," he said, his voice so full of ache that even as a self-centered, insensitive, spoiled little kid, I felt sorry for him. I wrapped my arms around his shoulders and gave him a big kiss on the cheek and I promised that I would never, ever, ever forget my helmet again.

Why didn't he tell me about Elizabeth then? Why didn't he tell me this summer, when Mom started crying all the time? Why didn't he tell me before we came to Sanderfield?

I want to believe that I now have all the puzzle pieces turned right side up, that figuring out my parents is just a matter of slipping the pieces into place. I can see Elizabeth's face taking form. (Hazily—I can't bear to think of her looking too much like me.) I can see why Mom would start crying on the anniversary of Elizabeth's birth and death, and why she would have trouble shaking her sorrow as I edge toward thirteen, the age Elizabeth was when she died. I'm a little creeped out about my birthday right now, myself. But why drive from Pennsylvania to Illinois? Why leave me with Myrlie? Why cancel our cell phone service? Why erase us from public information?

I remember an essay a kid in my English class wrote, that got a lot of attention. The title was something like "Teenagers Get a Bad Rap," and his whole point was that society is wrong to blame kids for becoming mouthy and irresponsible and impulsive and rebellious during their teen years. He argued that the true problem is that parents go psycho worrying about their kids.

"They force us to act the way we do, in self-defense," was one of his lines.

"My parents have always been psycho," I whisper into the darkness. "Because of Elizabeth. And because . . ."

But I can't finish my sentence, because there's still too much I don't know.

How much does Myrlie know?

—FIFTEEN—

It's nearly noon when I stumble down the stairs and into the kitchen the next morning. I'm still rubbing sleep from my eyes, trying to make them focus. My glasses bounce up and down, making my vision sharp and blurry, sharp and blurry. I slide into a chair across from Myrlie, who's sipping coffee and reading a new *Sanderfield Reporter.*

"Did Dad call again? Did I miss it?" I ask.

Myrlie puts down the paper.

"He hasn't called," she says. "How'd you sleep?"

"Okay, I guess," I say, because it's simpler than explaining that I feel like I had nightmares all night long, though I can't remember any of them now. I notice that she's still wearing her red bathrobe. "Did you take off work again?"

"It's Saturday," Myrlie says.

"Oh." I feel stupid. I was able to keep track of the days back home, but I did more than change time zones when I came to

Sanderfield. I slipped into an alternate universe. How was I to know that the days of the week stayed the same?

"I've been thinking," Myrlie says, leaning across the table. "Now that you know about Elizabeth, I think you should meet Joss."

"Joss? Your daughter?" I don't know why I say that like a question. Every word Myrlie spoke to me last night is firmly engrained in my memory. I could just as easily recite, like a reference-robot: "Joss Wilker. Born August 1978 to Myrlie and Thomas Wilker. Child gymnast and best friend of her cousin Elizabeth. Survived June 1991 accident that killed Elizabeth and Joss's father. Hospitalized for a long time afterward." Suddenly, I realize that I don't know much about Joss since 1991, except that she's the one who recommended that Myrlie buy her hybrid gas-electric car. And she isn't married.

"Yes, Joss, my daughter," Myrlie says. "She lives over in St. Louis, so she doesn't get back to visit too often. But . . . you are cousins. You should know one another."

Myrlie has such a hopeful look on her face, I can't tell her that I don't feel like meeting anyone.

"All right," I say. I'm having a hard time remembering that Joss is a grown-up now, as old as Tammy at the Y with her little girl and her pregnant belly.

Someone else to be amazed by how much I look like Elizabeth, I think. I don't like looking like Elizabeth—I wish she'd had dark hair and dark eyes and had taken after some entirely opposite branch of the family.

"What does Joss do?" I ask, trying to distract myself. I have a feeling she never made it to the '92 Olympics, either, or Myrlie would have said so. Maybe I would have even heard of her. But I'm still picturing her as a tiny gymnast in a leotard.

"Oh, she's a minister," Myrlie says. "She'll have to preach tomorrow morning, so she can't come today. But she usually has Mondays off, so she could probably come tomorrow afternoon and spend the night. I'll give her a call a little later."

I'm trying to mentally replace the gymnast's leotard with a liturgical robe, and it's not working very well. I glance down at the newspaper on the table to distract myself. Today's *Sanderfield Reporter* has yet another article about the Chicago embezzler, and something else about the President. It's weird that the newspaper is still reporting the same news, when my whole world changed overnight.

"Now. Would you prefer breakfast or lunch?" Myrlie asks. "Since it's eleven fifty-two, I think you have your choice."

"Breakfast," I say. "I can get it."

I walk to the cupboard where I saw Myrlie put the Raisin Bran the day before. Now it's got company: a yellow box of Corn Pops and a red box of Froot Loops. I grab the Froot Loops and carry it over to Myrlie at arm's length, as if it's evidence in a criminal case.

"How did you know?" I ask. "How did you know I'd like Froot Loops?"

Myrlie looks troubled, probably because I'm practically shouting at her.

"I didn't," she said. "It was just a guess. Elizabeth always loved Froot Loops, and I don't know, you just remind me so much of her, it made me feel good to buy Froot Loops for you. I figured if you didn't like them, I could always donate the box to charity."

"Elizabeth must not have liked nuts, huh?" I say. I try to remember what else Myrlie had seemed to know too easily about me the day before, when she was making her grocery list. "And she must have loved blueberry muffins, and peaches-and-cream oatmeal. . . ."

"Right," Myrlie says. "Yesterday when I was asking you what you liked and didn't like, I suddenly felt like you *were* Elizabeth and she'd come back and I was getting a chance to feed her. . . . I'm sorry. This is probably sounding too strange to you. Am I making you uncomfortable? Probably some food preferences are genetic, and you inherited some of the same genes as her. Then, too, Hillary would have cooked the same foods for you that she cooked for Elizabeth. . . . And it's not like you like everything the same, not if you hate peaches-and-cream oatmeal. Elizabeth *loved* that. She'd choose it over chocolate."

"Really?" I don't tell Myrlie I lied yesterday. But I put the box of Froot Loops back in the cupboard and eat the Corn Pops instead. They're too hard and too sweet and too full of puffed air. I eat a whole bowlful and still feel totally empty inside.

—SIXTEEN—

My father doesn't call again the entire rest of the day.

"Maybe he thought that call in the middle of the night counted as today's call," Myrlie says.

We're in front of the TV watching the evening news, something Myrlie says she tries to do every day. This strikes me as odd, since my parents never watch the news, never read the newspaper. Maybe Dad checks out the events of the day online, when he's working, but if he does he never tells me or Mom about it. It's as if my parents would like to forget the rest of the world exists.

I don't want to think about my parents, or the reasons my father hasn't called. I concentrate on the TV. The newscaster's talking about that embezzler who just got out of prison. Dalton Van Dyne's his name.

"Six million dollars disappeared from Digispur during Van

Dyne's tenure as CEO," the newscaster says. "Most of the money has never been found."

I'm thinking that the big words used in the news—tenure, embezzler—sound like they should be fun, but they have such boring meanings. "Embezzler" should be someone who goes around buzzing a kazoo all the time. Not someone who steals money.

Myrlie sighs.

"Crime is so complicated nowadays," she says. "Did I tell you my husband was a lawyer? He always said it was scary how stupid most criminals were. I guess they have to be smarter now." She gets a faraway look in her eye. "I remember when Tom and I got engaged, my parents were so proud because they were going to have a doctor and a lawyer as sons-in-law. It's funny, how stuff like that used to matter so much."

I'm busy trying to think of a more imaginative definition for "tenure," so I almost miss the news hidden in Myrlie's reminiscing. Then it registers.

"Wait a minute," I say. "My dad was your parents' other son-in-law. Dad's not a doctor."

Myrlie gives me a baffled look.

"He *was*," she says.

I try to picture my father as a guy in a white coat or green scrubs. It's easier to imagine him blowing a kazoo.

"He's a money manager," I say. "He sits at the computer all day long."

Myrlie opens her mouth to disagree, as if we're playing some childish game of "I know Walter Cole better than you know Walter Cole." Then she seems to reconsider.

"Maybe," she says carefully, "it was too hard for him to

continue in medicine after what happened to Elizabeth. Too hard to watch other children die. I seem to remember Hillary saying something about him maybe switching into medical research—I guess even that hit a little too close to home."

Myrlie turns back to the TV, but I don't.

"When did Mom say that?" I ask.

"At Elizabeth's funeral, probably. Or Tom's? That time period is just such a blur in my mind. . . . I do remember thinking it must have had to do with them donating Elizabeth's organs. They were able to keep her alive for a few hours after the accident, so someone else could benefit. Maybe that inspired Walter somehow."

"Really?" I say. This changes how I've been thinking about Elizabeth. It makes everything worse. Not only do I have a dead sister I never heard about before last night, but her heart and lungs and kidneys and other organs—her eyes?—are still alive in other people's bodies. This is like one of those late-night horror movies Mom and Dad never let me watch.

Myrlie punches a button on the remote control to turn off the TV.

"Are you okay?" she asks. "I didn't mean to upset you."

Upset. That's the same word Dad had used as an excuse for not telling me about Elizabeth.

"I'm fine," I lie.

Myrlie's still looking at me doubtfully.

"I wouldn't blame you if you were upset," she says.

I shrug, and Myrlie seems to get the message.

"So Walter's a money manager, now," she says.

"Yes. The past few years, he's mostly worked from home. He's semiretired." I try to make it sound ordinary and dull. I want ordinary and dull rather desperately right now.

"I'm sure Hillary appreciates that. You too," Myrlie says. "I know that was one of Walter's regrets, that he was away so much when Elizabeth was a child. He always said if he had it to do all over again . . ."

Her voice trails off. I think about how my father is always there, waiting, when I get home from school. I think about how, when I was little, he and Mom both tucked me into bed every single night. I think about how he helped me with my homework, let me braid beads into his thinning hair, let me win at Candyland and Trouble.

And I think about how he's as good as vanished from the face of the Earth since the last time I talked to him.

—SEVENTEEN—

Somehow I manage to sleep through the night, survive into another day. At the breakfast table, Myrlie is fidgety.

"Do you think . . . ?" she begins. "I mean, if it's all right with you . . ."

"What?" I say, even though my mouth is full of coffee cake. Myrlie got up early and baked this morning.

"I would like to go to church this morning," Myrlie says. "I need to."

Going to church is something else my parents don't do—like watching TV news or reading the newspaper. Or telling me about long-lost relatives I never knew I had.

"Why?" I say. "Oh—because your daughter's a minister and it would look bad if you skipped? Does she keep track of whether or not you go?" I'm a little amused at this notion. Myrlie laughs too.

"It's not like that," she says. "It's more that . . . this has been an emotionally wrenching couple of days for me, too. Church always makes me feel better. More focused on what really matters."

If my parents went to church, would that have prevented them from dumping me on Myrlie? Would it have prevented them from disappearing?

"So, go," I say brusquely.

"Do you want to go with me?" Myrlie asks.

I wince.

"That woman from the Y—Tammy—does she go to your church?"

Myrlie tilts her head to the side, her eyes full of compassion.

"No," she says.

"Would there be anybody else there who would look at me and remember Elizabeth?"

"I don't know," Myrlie says. "Elizabeth never had glasses like yours, so that kind of . . . hides the resemblance. Tammy saw you without them. And you're a lot taller than Elizabeth was until right at the end, those last few months. I'm sure everyone remembers her as being a tiny little thing. It's funny how she was always so petite, and then it was like her body suddenly decided, 'Oops— I'm supposed to be taking after my six-feet-four father instead of my five-feet-one mother.' She went from being the shortest on her gymnastics team to the tallest practically overnight."

I get chills as Myrlie chatters away, because she might as well be describing my own growth spurt. I went from being the shortest to the tallest in my age category on my swim team. Coach Dinkle changed my nickname on the team roster from "Water Bug" to "Giant Mermaid."

Elizabeth was your sister. It's not surprising that you followed the same growth pattern, I tell myself.

Myrlie clears her throat. I guess I've gone a long time without answering.

"You know, it shouldn't matter if people recognize you or not," she says. "Now that you know about Elizabeth, I can introduce you as my niece. You can meet people who knew your parents when they were your age."

I shake my head, not even tempted.

"I should stay here in case my dad calls," I say.

"He could leave a message," she says. "Or call back. You shouldn't feel . . . trapped here."

"I don't," I say, which is another lie.

Myrlie doesn't look like she believes me, but she bustles about changing her clothes, gathering together her coat and her purse and her Bible.

The phone rings as soon as she's gone.

"Daddy, why didn't you call yesterday?" I ask before I even say hello.

Click.

I feel my face get red. Obviously other people besides my father might have reason to call Myrlie. It just seems odd that whoever this was didn't bother to say anything.

I've just hung up the phone when it rings again.

"Hello?"

"Bethany?"

This time it is my father.

"Dad, I waited all day yesterday for you to call—"

"We've had some . . . complications," he says, his voice sounding strained and anxious. "I can't talk for long, and

I'm not sure when I'll be able to call back again. Is Myrlie there?"

I'm stung. He hasn't seen me in two and a half days, and he's barely bothered to say hello.

"She went to church," I say. "She'll be back at eleven thirty."

"She left you alone?" he asks, sounding panicked.

"Daddy, I'm twelve years old. Lots of kids my age stay by themselves for hours. Some even babysit."

"This is different," he says. "Tell Myrlie she needs to keep you with her all the time."

"Mmm," I say, because I'm not sure I'm going to tell her that or not. I change the subject. "Daddy, she told me about Elizabeth." I'm a little angry with my parents right now, but, still, I wonder if I should offer some condolences, some sympathy.

"I'm sorry," my father says, as if I'm the one overcome with grief for this sister I never met. "It would have been better if you'd never had to know."

"Never?" I say, the anger rising again. How ignorant did he want me to be? Before Thursday night, had he ever thought about introducing me to Myrlie? Had he ever planned to show me Sanderfield, his and Mom's hometown? How could he have kept such a huge chunk of their lives secret from me?

And why had he wanted to?

"Bethany," he says. "There's a lot you don't understand. A lot you *can't* understand. This isn't the way I wanted everything to play out. I'm doing the best I can."

The pleading in his voice is so bald, I feel my anger ebb.

"Okay," I say, trying for steadiness. "But when are you coming back?"

"I don't know," he says. "Everything has changed. Be strong."

That's something my father has never asked of me. Before now, my parents just expected me to be cute and cuddly and entertaining. And happy. They wanted my happiness most of all.

What changed?

Everything . . .

"Tell Myrlie I'll call her back later," my father is saying. "We need to talk about arrangements for you and school. We can't have you falling behind."

It's only after we've both hung up that I realize what that means. If Dad's worried about school, this isn't just a two- or three-day jaunt, a minivacation from my typical life. This is long-term.

"I bet they never did anything like this to Elizabeth," I mutter into the silence of Myrlie's house.

—EIGHTEEN—

When Myrlie comes home, she's in a good mood. We have a quick lunch and then she scurries around getting ready for Joss's visit. I tell her that Dad called and will call again, but I don't say anything about school or her needing to keep me by her side at all times. Dad can tell her that himself, if he wants to so badly.

"Okay, good. I'm glad you won't have to keep worrying about him," Myrlie says, but she's concentrating on polishing the huge antique mirror in the hallway. "Can you hand me the Windex?"

I pick up the bottle of blue liquid. She switches to cleaning the window in the front door.

"Is Joss some kind of a neat freak?" I ask.

Myrlie laughs.

"No, but I used to be, and I always think Joss might expect to see everything the way it was when she was a kid."

"I thought you lived in a house around the corner." It bothers me that there might have been some holes in Myrlie's story. What if I can't trust her either?

"Joss and I moved here after the accident," Myrlie says, still scrubbing. "We moved in with my mother."

"I have a grandmother?" I look around, almost as if I'm expecting some super-old granny to come popping out. Some other relative my parents hadn't bothered telling me about.

Myrlie lowers her Windex bottle.

"Mom died the following winter," she says. "That was really a horrible year for us."

"Did my parents come back for her funeral?" I ask.

Myrlie hesitates, then shakes her head. No.

"I suspect it was too hard for them, coming so soon after Elizabeth's," she says.

"But you went, right?"

"I did," she says. "I wanted to. And Tom was supposed to be the executor of her estate—she'd never changed that in her will—so the job fell to me. I handled all the details. I was experienced by then. I was used to dealing with death."

I'm not sure what it means to be executor of an estate, but it sounds hard-edged and businesslike. Heartless. Doubly difficult for someone in mourning.

And meanwhile my parents were AWOL, just like they were now.

"Bethany," Myrlie says softly. "All that happened a long time ago." She goes back to scrubbing windows. "It is a shame that you never got to meet your grandmother, though. She doted on her grandchildren."

Joss and Elizabeth, I think. *Not me.*

By the time Joss shows up, Myrlie has the house in perfect order, and, in spite of myself, I'm a little curious about what Joss will be like.

If she looks like me too, I'm just going to scream, I think.

But as Joss lets herself in the front door, calling out, "Hello? Anyone home?" I discover she's a younger, thinner, darker, and more intense version of Myrlie, all sharp elbows and knees where Myrlie is padded and round. Joss is also wearing a sweatshirt with rolled-up sleeves and jeans with a hole in the knee, which really shatters my image of what a minister should look like.

Myrlie rushes out of the kitchen, gives Joss a hug, and surrounds her in a flurry of questions. "Was there much traffic? How'd your sermon go this morning? Are you hungry?"

Then they both seem to remember me.

"Bethany?" Myrlie calls.

I scramble up from the couch where I've been half-hiding, feeling awkward and out of place.

"There you are," Myrlie says, beaming. "Joss, this is Bethany. Bethany, this is Joss."

Joss looks at me and for a second I see the same mix of surprise and awe and shock and horror that showed up in Myrlie's face when she first met me, and in Tammy's face when she saw me at the Y. Then Joss smiles, hiding her first reaction.

"Glad to meet you," she says, and she sounds so sincere I want to believe her. She shakes my hand, and that almost makes me feel like a grown-up.

Minutes later, we're all back in the kitchen with Myrlie. I never knew preparing a meal for three people could take so much effort. I'm slicing onions and Myrlie is shredding cheese and Joss is talking about a member of her church who told her on the way out of the sanctuary today, "Well, you certainly, um, used a lot of words in your sermon today."

"What did he expect—hand signals? American Sign Language?" Joss asks indignantly as she tears lettuce for our salad.

"He probably didn't mean anything by it," Myrlie says. "He just didn't think. You don't know what might be going on in his life right now."

"I know, I know, I should use his rudeness as an occasion to grow my own compassion," Joss says, sighing. "I will—later. I just need to vent right now."

"You don't want Bethany to get a bad impression of you," Myrlie says.

"Why not?" Joss says. "Better that she knows what I'm like right away. Here it is, Bethany, I'll tell you now: I'm the black sheep of the family."

"I thought you were a minister," I squeak out.

Joss laughs.

"Ah, but I'm in the wrong church, according to my mother. And the wrong city, because St. Louis is much, much too far away. And she probably would have been happier if I'd gotten married about ten years ago and cranked out two-point-three adorable grandchildren. And—"

"Joss, stop!" Myrlie is laughing again. "You know I'm very proud of you."

Joss shrugs and rolls her eyes at me and I think it's kind of nice, after all, having a cousin.

"Why did you become a minister?" I ask, sliding my onions into the sauce Myrlie has bubbling on the stove.

Joss stops tearing lettuce and glances quickly at her mother. Myrlie nods, almost imperceptibly.

"The year I was thirteen," Joss begins, "I spent a lot of time grappling with God and trying to understand life and death. After the accident, you know. And then it just seemed like it would have been a big waste not to put all that theological thought to use."

"Because you figured out all the answers?" I ask.

"Hardly," Joss says wryly. "I just figured out all the questions. I don't think there was a single one I missed asking God."

She dumps her lettuce into a salad spinner and the next thing I know we're talking about movies and books and TV shows—safe topics. As we finish cooking and sit down to eat, I can tell Myrlie and Joss are steering the conversation away from anything controversial. They're trying to make me feel comfortable. I'm simultaneously touched and relieved and a little bit insulted.

Don't they think I can handle talking about anything important? I wonder. *Anything that hits a little closer to home than the new remake of* The Parent Trap?

We eat Myrlie's pasta and homemade bread and salad, and she clears away the dishes. Then there's a lull in the conversation as she brings out the chocolate cake she made this afternoon. I turn to Joss and say, "What was it like growing up with Elizabeth?"

Joss raises an eyebrow at me and glances at her mother again.

"Go ahead," Myrlie says quietly.

Joss shifts in her chair.

"You might as well ask me what it was like to grow up," Joss says. "I can't imagine what my childhood would have been like without Elizabeth."

"You were twelve when she died," I say.

"And as far as I'm concerned, that was the end of my childhood," Joss says. She peers at me so intently it's all I can do to keep from looking away. But I want her to see I'm not afraid of hearing about Elizabeth.

"Elizabeth was a lot of fun," Myrlie says, putting a slice of cake down in front of me. "Full of energy. Those two girls did nothing but giggle when they were together."

Joss gives Myrlie a look I can't quite read. She turns back to me.

"Do you want to hear a eulogy?" she asks me. "One of those 'We won't speak ill of the dead—what a saint she was' descriptions? Or do you want the warts-and-all version of Elizabeth's life?"

"Warts and all," I say. I swallow hard. "Part of me really wants to hate Elizabeth. Because she belonged to my parents before I did. Because she . . ." I almost say, "ruined them," but how can I blame Elizabeth for her own death? "Because she had them when they were younger and happier."

I'm a little surprised I've allowed myself to be so honest. But something about Joss's gaze seems to make it safe.

Joss gives me a sympathetic smile.

"Part of me always wanted to hate Elizabeth too," she says. "Especially after she died. Can't miss someone you hate, right? But even before, when she was still alive . . . Elizabeth was always prettier and smarter than me. She was a better gymnast too. It was like she had a huge advantage, being born two months ahead of me. She walked before I did and talked before I did. She learned how to read before I did. She was better at everything."

"Joss!" Myrlie sounds scandalized. "You know that's not true. Elizabeth wasn't any prettier or smarter than you. And you were just as good at gymnastics. Even better sometimes, especially toward the end—"

"I'm just saying how I felt at the time," Joss interjects. "And it's really not fair to compare our gymnastics abilities those last few months, after Elizabeth grew so quickly. It really threw her off, being so tall all of a sudden. I think she would have adjusted, if she'd had more time."

I decide I'm glad my sport is swimming, where height doesn't matter. And then I remember something I hadn't thought about in years. When I was in first or second grade, we'd done a gymnastics unit in school, and the teacher had been impressed at how quickly I'd picked it up. She said I had "a lot of natural ability"—a phrase that stuck with me because I thought it had to do with nature, and I kept imagining myself with vines and leaves growing all over me as I did somersaults. I can remember feeling proud when the teacher sent a note home with me recommending that I take gymnastics lessons. Maybe I was hoping to grow leaves, even though I had to have known that was childish and silly.

Anyhow, my parents had said no, absolutely not. No gymnastics for me.

That was because of Elizabeth, I realize now. At the time I hadn't cared that much, because when they refused to let me do gymnastics, they let me join a swim team instead. I probably started daydreaming about growing fins, not leaves. But now I think, *Natural ability?* That's practically the same term Myrlie had used to describe Joss and Elizabeth's gymnastics talents. *Naturals, people said . . .*

"Apart from their little rivalries—which, I admit, Hillary and I probably didn't help—Joss and Elizabeth *were* best friends," Myrlie says, and I'm grateful for the distraction.

"Sure. Worst of enemies and best of friends all rolled into one," Joss says, taking a bite of her cake. "Ever see those athlete personality profiles they do during the Olympics? Elizabeth and I spent hours figuring out how ours would sound." She lowers her voice and imitates a self-important sports announcer: "'In a tiny town in the middle of nowhere, Illinois, not one but two talented young gymnasts harbored Olympic dreams. Cousins Jocelyn Wilker and Elizabeth Krull'—we were always debating about whose name should come first. *I* always said it should be by age, youngest to oldest, and Elizabeth always said it should be alphabetical, Krull before Wilker—"

"Wait a minute. Krull?" I say. "Not 'Cole'?"

Joss looks over at her mother.

"Oops," she says.

—NINETEEN—

I look from my cousin to my aunt—that is, assuming they really are my cousin and my aunt, assuming I can believe anything I've been told since I left Pennsylvania three days ago.

"Joss, you weren't supposed to say anything about that," Myrlie says. "Not until I have a chance to ask Walter—"

"What, you have to get his permission to talk?" Joss asks.

"I promised I'd protect Bethany," Myrlie says. "She's only twelve."

"The same age I was when I lost my entire family," Joss says.

"You still had me," Myrlie says.

"I might as well have lost you, too, that first year or so."

"I know. I was kind of . . . emotionally absent. I'm sorry."

They have a strange way of arguing, their voices getting softer and slower instead of louder and angrier, their points of view getting closer together instead of farther apart. But it's like they've forgotten I'm even there.

"What are you protecting me from?" I demand.

Myrlie and Joss look at one another and Myrlie shrugs.

"I don't know," Myrlie says apologetically. "Your dad said to keep you safe, and Thursday night I thought that just meant the basics. Food and shelter and compassion while your mother was . . ."

"Having a breakdown," I say. "Going crazy."

Myrlie frowns, but she doesn't correct me.

"Why was Elizabeth's last name different from mine?" I persist.

"She had the same last name as her parents," Myrlie says. "Elizabeth Krull, Walter and Hillary Krull—"

"Their name is Cole," I say stubbornly. "*Cole.* You heard me say that on the phone Thursday night."

"It didn't register then," Myrlie says. "Cole and Krull sound so much alike, and I was feeling a little . . . overwhelmed. I didn't know you had a different last name until Friday at the Y when you spelled it for Ronald Boesdorfer's mom. I wanted to ask your dad about it before I said anything to you. Just in case. But I haven't had much of a chance to talk to Walter. So I was going to be . . ."—she glares at Joss—"discreet."

Joss ignores the glare and leans forward.

"Why would Aunt Hillary and Uncle Walter change their *name*?" she asks. "Bethany, as far as you know, has your last name always been Cole?"

"Yeah," I say, but suddenly I'm not so sure. I squint, trying to focus on a vague memory of being a little kid sitting in a too-large, too-stiff chair in front of a too-cheerful man in some official place—a bank or an insurance office, maybe a car dealership. The man's handing my dad a stack of papers, saying, "I think that will be everything, Mr. and Mrs. . . ." Had he said "Cole"? Or had it been "Burns" or "Stern" or something like that? "I think," I tell Myrlie and Joss.

"Uncle Walter and Aunt Hillary using an alias—it's kind of hard to imagine," Joss says.

I turn to Myrlie.

"Don't try to protect me," I say. "Tell me the truth."

"The truth is, I haven't understood anything about Walter and Hillary since June 13, 1991," Myrlie says. She holds her hands out, palms up, a gesture of innocence. "I'm as puzzled as you are."

It's impossible not to believe Myrlie. It's impossible to look at her kind, troubled, sympathetic face and not feel a little comforted. Even if I do feel like I've been zapped into the Twilight Zone.

A name's a pretty basic thing, Mom and Dad, I think. *Why wouldn't you even tell me about that?*

"Well," Joss says, because we've all fallen silent, staring bleakly at the cake we no longer have any appetite for. "Where's Uncle Walter's phone number? I'm going to call him right now, clear this all up."

"He didn't leave a number," Myrlie says. "Bethany and I are just supposed to wait for his calls."

Joss lets out an exasperated snort.

"Come on, Mom," she says. "You were a lawyer's wife. Weren't you worried about liability issues? At the church, we have to have people sign all sorts of legal forms just to leave their kids with us for a couple hours of preschool twice a week.

Uncle Walter gave you Bethany for who knows how long and he didn't leave you a phone number? If there was an emergency, you wouldn't even be allowed to authorize medical treatment for her."

"You know me," Myrlie says. "I wasn't thinking about liability. I was worried about Hillary and Walter. And Bethany."

Myrlie reaches out and puts her hand on my shoulder, draws me toward her.

She is my aunt. Joss is my cousin. I'm sure of it. But the longer I'm in Sanderfield, the less I know about my parents.

—TWENTY—

Myrlie releases me from her hug. She and Joss carry off plates and glasses, scrape our half-eaten cake slices into the trash. They stand at the sink washing and drying dishes.

I don't move. I am frozen in place at the table.

Joss comes and sits across from me. She lowers her head so her eyes peer directly into mine.

"What can we do?" she asks. "How can we help?"

Find my parents, I want to say. *Make them act normal. Make them tell me the truth. The whole truth. Give me answers.*

I remember that Joss claims to know more about questions than answers. I swallow hard.

"Tell me the rest of your story," I say. "About you and Elizabeth making up your personality profiles for the Olympics."

Joss looks relieved that I'm asking for something she can deliver. Or maybe she's just happy that I'm still capable of talking.

"I can do better than that," Joss says. "I can show you the profiles we acted out. We begged and begged and forced Dad and Uncle Walter to tape them—I'm sure Mom has some of those tapes around here somewhere." A shadow of something like doubt crosses her face. "That is, if you *want* to see those tapes."

"I do," I say, with more certainty than I feel. Ever since Myrlie told me about Elizabeth, I've avoided asking to see so much as a picture of her, even though I'm sure Myrlie has some of those lying around her house somewhere too. And now I'm agreeing to watch video of her walking and talking—fully alive?

Be strong, I tell myself, and it bothers me that those are the same words my father used.

The videotapes, it turns out, are in the closet of an unused bedroom upstairs. It takes all three of us to shift around the dusty boxes, dig in past the fraying cardboard flaps. While we're looking for the tapes, we find one whole box full of Joss's old gymnastics trophies and ribbons.

"You were such a star," Myrlie says wistfully, a touch of awe in her voice as she stares down at the still-shiny statuettes. "You *could* have gone to the Olympics."

"It didn't matter to me after the accident," Joss says impatiently. "It wasn't worth it without Elizabeth."

I feel like I'm hearing a replay of an old argument.

Elizabeth must have had a box of trophies like this, too, I think. *Wonder what Mom and Dad did with them?* I think about our many moves. We had boxes that just traveled from the attic in one house to the basement of another. Were some of those boxes full of Elizabeth's belongings? Would I have found out about Elizabeth all by myself, back home, if I'd just showed a bit more curiosity, nosed around a little?

No, I think bitterly. *Mom or Dad would never have let me out of their sight long enough to discover anything on my own.*

Still, I suppress a shiver, that I might have been so close to everything Elizabeth left behind, just one floor away my entire life.

Joss pulls on a box that promptly tears apart in her hands, spilling out old-fashioned videotapes. She barely manages to catch a monstrous, old-style camcorder that slides out of the top of the box.

"Good grief, Mom," Joss says in exaggerated disgust. "Didn't you ever read the passage in the Bible about not storing up your treasures where dust and moth can consume them?"

"Yeah, Ms. Smartmouth Preacher, and I know the point of that passage is about aiming toward heaven, not spending a fortune at the Container Store," Myrlie says, giving Joss a playful swat on the shoulder.

"But this is my childhood, disintegrating before my eyes," Joss says, still in a tone of mock disgust.

"I'm glad you can joke about these things now," Myrlie says softly, turning toward Joss. Their eyes lock, and I feel like an outsider again for a moment. I can only guess at the undercurrent of emotion beneath their banter. If I'd had a childhood like Joss's—with the same tragic end—would I want to keep all the mementos?

Joss glances my way, then back at her mother.

"Seriously, Mom, you should think about transferring all these tapes to DVD, before they completely fall apart," she says.

"You're welcome to take on that chore," Myrlie says.

"Ah, I'm too busy feeding the hungry, visiting the sick, preaching to the nonbelievers," Joss says. "Especially Mr. You Used a Lot of Words Today."

"And I've got my hands full right now trying to teach Anthony Doulin the alphabet," Myrlie says, grinning.

"Maybe I could make the DVDs for you," I say, and the other two turn to me in surprise. I swallow hard. "I mean, if I'm here very long, I could. I'm actually pretty good with electronics."

And then I prove my boast by being the only one who can figure how to hook up the camcorder to the unwieldy old VCR that Myrlie also has to dig out of a closet. It makes me feel smart and capable and in control for the first time since I left home.

"Ah, the wisdom of the younger generation," Joss jokes. "Born with a remote control in each hand—what would we do without you?"

"We couldn't watch these videotapes, that's what," Myrlie says, settling into a corner of the couch.

"You could have just asked one of your kindergarteners to come over and set up everything for you. Offered them extra credit," Joss says.

"And have them find out how stupid I am?" Myrlie says. "No way."

The joking stops as soon as I cue up the tape we've plucked out of the box labeled 1990. Myrlie inhales sharply, and Joss clutches her hand.

Behind the flashing block showing the date and time—2:04 P.M., August 5, 1990—there's a man on the screen. He's a few inches too short to be the proverbial tall, dark, and handsome, but he's nice-looking in a middle-aged kind of way. He's sitting on a couch reading a newspaper. The *Sanderfield Reporter*, I notice.

"Dad," Joss explains, unnecessarily.

Tom Wilker doesn't seem to know he's being taped. He turns a page of the newspaper.

"Here we are," a girl's voice whispers from out of range of the camera, in the manner of nature documentaries. "Stalking that rare creature, Mayorus Sanderfieldus in his native habitat."

The sound is so distorted, I can't tell if the voice is Joss's or not. Do people sound the same at eleven or twelve as they do as adults?

"You doofus!" Another voice says. "He's not in his *native* habitat. We're at Grandma's. And he's not just *rare*. He's unique. One of a kind. He's the only sitting mayor of Sanderfield. All the others would be Mayorus Sanderfieldus Emeritus."

Somehow I know this is Elizabeth. Her voice even sounds a little like mine, when I'm being smart-alecky.

"Would that change if he stood up? Get it? Sitting mayor? Standing up?" Is that Joss—standing up to Elizabeth?

Both girls crack up, their laughter providing a kind of soundtrack as Tom lowers his newspaper and smiles toward the camera.

"Hi, girls. What are you up to?" he asks lazily, a man who doesn't know he's got less than a year to live.

"Since all you adults are too *busy* to tape us, we decided we'd tape you," Joss says on the video.

"I was *such* a brat," the adult Joss says beside me. "How'd you guys put up with me?"

"We loved you," Myrlie says.

"Yeah, but why was I a brat on tape?" Joss asked. "This might ruin my chances of ever being elevated to Pope."

"You're not Catholic," Myrlie says, laughing.

I guess they've gotten over the shock of seeing their deceased husband/father on the TV screen. I don't know how they can joke around like that. And I've missed some of the conversation on the tape.

"Yes, this is manipulation and blackmail of a public official," Elizabeth is saying now. "What are you going to do—arrest us?"

"No! I'm going to . . ."—Tom lunges toward the camera, his face suddenly eerily large; then the view swings around wildly, showing first the wood panels of the floor, then the maroon walls and the white ceiling—"steal the camera from you and film the best darn Olympic profile ever!"

The screen goes black.

"He fell for it," Joss says. She has tears in her eyes. "He always was a soft touch."

"For you," Myrlie agrees.

A picture reappears on the TV screen. This time it's two girls in red, white, and blue leotards standing on their hands in a huge expanse of grass. Joss and Elizabeth, one dark-haired, one blond. I can't see their faces because they have their backs to the camera, but I can tell how muscular their arms and legs are. They're perfectly matched and perfectly still, like statues, their toes pointed to the sky.

"I'm supposed to read this?" Tom's voice comes from behind the camera. One of them must have said yes, because he clears his throat and launches into, "In tiny Sanderfield, Illinois, population eighty-five hundred—hey, girls, you should make that eighty-five hundred and *one*, because Jody Smuckers had her baby last night and—"

"Daddy!" The voice is dim, but the outrage is clear.

"Okay, okay. I'll just go on." He makes his voice sound pompous, like a TV newscaster. "Two girls, cousins and best of friends, showed athletic promise at a very young age. Elizabeth Krull turned somersaults in her crib. Jocelyn Wilker began practicing cartwheels at age three. And now, after years of hard work and dedication, they're fulfilling that early promise at the Olympics."

The two statues/gymnasts explode into motions, turning the handstands into back walkovers, round-offs, leaps, and spins.

"Aren't they amazing, folks?" Tom Wilker asks.

The screen goes dark again, and then the scene changes. The camera is moving toward a house—the very house I'm sitting in now, I realize. But the house looks different because it's summertime on the screen, and everything is green and lush. A riot of petunias and marigolds and pansies and geraniums line the sidewalk and spill out from hanging baskets on the porch. The two girls are in shorts and T-shirts now, and they're sitting on a wicker porch swing hanging near the front door. I feel a pang, remembering how that first night I'd imagined the porch as a setting for an early-1900s happy-family movie. It *had* been the scene of happy times, but it'd been in the late 1900s, and the happy family had been Joss and Elizabeth, Myrlie and Tom, Mom and Dad.

"We caught up with the two girls recently at their grandmother's house to talk to them about their brilliant careers," Tom narrates as he walks the camera up the porch steps and toward the girls. "Hi, girls!"

"Hi," they both say, and there's a scraping noise that must be Tom pulling up a chair. The camera zooms in and goes temporarily fuzzy.

"How'd the two of you get interested in gymnastics?" Tom asks.

"Well, we always liked being active." It's Elizabeth's voice. The camera zooms in closer, swinging even further out of focus. "Our moms started us in dance lessons when we were three years old. But that was so . . . *sedentary.*" I hear Joss giggling in the background, on-screen. Elizabeth pauses to glare at her cousin, then goes on. "Then in 1984 . . ."

I don't hear the rest of what Elizabeth is saying, because the camera is finally in focus. Elizabeth's face fills the whole TV screen, and I can see every freckle, every light hair of her eyelashes and eyebrows. And the freckles are just like mine, a light smattering across the bridge of her nose, a few more on the right check than the left. The eyelashes and eyebrows are just like mine, wispy and hard to see. The nose and eyes and mouth and heart-shaped face structure are the same too. The only way I can tell I'm not just looking in a mirror is that Elizabeth isn't wearing glasses, and she has braces on her teeth.

I got my braces off last year.

I gasp. Myrlie reaches over and takes my hand.

"Should we stop the tape?" Joss asks.

"No," I murmur weakly. *This isn't too strange—we're sisters,* I tell myself. *Sisters look alike. Like Mom and Myrlie. Mary-Kate and Ashley Olsen from that old TV show* Full House. *Okay, they're twins. How about my friend . . . ?* But I can't think of any friends—or even acquaintances—who look so much like their sisters. *Elizabeth and I are identical except for the glasses.*

"Look how much Elizabeth is blinking," Myrlie says. "Remember how determined she was that those contacts were going to work out?"

Oh, I think, and it's like I've had yet another bombshell dropped on me.

But I force myself to keep watching the TV screen, and I notice a few, small differences. Elizabeth has a tiny scar just above her lips, that gives her whole face a mischievous look. Her eyes light up and she bounces in her seat while she talks, as if it's impossible for her to keep all her energy and enthusiasm bottled up. I don't think I've ever looked that self-confident and unguarded, even in the days before Mom started crying full-time.

"And what do you like to do in your spare time? Besides gymnastics?" Tom asks from behind the camera.

"Oh, we don't have spare time," Joss says, and Tom swings the camera toward her. "We don't even have time to do our homework, except in the car on the way to gymnastics. It's always practice, practice, practice. We have to work really hard."

Up close, eleven-year-old Joss's face shocks me nearly as much as Elizabeth's. Joss looks not just smaller and younger, but unformed somehow, as if the pieces that are going to come together to make the grown-up Joss aren't all there yet. Her dark eyes seem a little vacant, and she seems to be trying too hard to be as enthusiastic and peppy as Elizabeth.

"Yes, we do practice a lot, but *I* have other interests besides gymnastics," Elizabeth says, and Tom focuses the camera back on her. "I like to run and paint and read and watch TV and go to movies. In fact, when I grow up and I'm too old to be a gymnast,

I'm going to go to Hollywood and be a set designer. Either that, or be a raconteur. That's someone who tells stories."

Beside me, Joss laughs.

"I'd almost forgotten how much Elizabeth liked using big words that nobody else knew," she says. "I mean, *raconteur?* From a twelve year old?"

Myrlie chuckles too, and neither of them seem to notice that I've gone stiff with horror. *I'm the one who wants to be a movie set designer,* I think. *I'm the one who likes to collect unusual words.* In fact, "raconteur," is exactly the kind of word I would have added to my list, though it's ruined for me now.

Is it because Elizabeth and I were raised by the same parents? I wonder. *Did they do something to make both of us love words and movies?*

As if on cue, I hear my mother's voice from the TV.

"Girls! Where are you?" she calls in the distance. "Time to go home!"

"And here are the parents of the two gymnastics prodigies," Tom says turning the camera toward Mom's voice. "Walter and Hillary Krull, and Myrlie Wilker and her husband—hmm, can't think where her husband could have gotten to. Tell the viewers of America: What's it like to have such talented daughters?"

"Exhausting!"

I think that's Myrlie's voice, but once again, the camera is taking a long time to focus, so it's hard to tell. Three blurry people are stepping out of the front door onto the porch—one tall, two short.

And then the focus finally kicks in and I see my parents and Myrlie as they used to be. They all look so young it's tempting to think of them as kids as well. None of them have any wrinkles;

Mom and Myrlie both have blond hair as radiant as Elizabeth's; my dad isn't stooped over at all but stands tall and straight and proud, with a full head of longish, sandy-colored hair. An older, white-haired woman joins them at the door. *The real Myrlie*, I think—but no, it's the grandmother, passing out good-bye hugs and calling out, "Come for Sunday dinner next week too! Same time!" I hear Elizabeth, off-camera, asking, "Mom, can Joss come home with us?" and then Joss complaining, "Dad! You don't need to tape *this*. The profile's over."

"Oh, all right," he says agreeably, and the screen goes black, then turns to fuzz.

The real-life, present-day, adult Joss sighs beside me.

"I wish he'd taped it all," she says. "Every single second."

She hits a button on the remote, shutting off the TV, and the three of us blink, resurfacing from the past.

—TWENTY·ONE—

We don't really talk about the video. Myrlie and Joss seem a little lost in their memories, and I'm struggling to act normal while carrying on an internal debate. *She didn't look that much like me. . . . Yes, she did. . . . No, she didn't. . . .*

"Want to play cards or something?" Joss finally says.

Myrlie and I both shrug, but that's all the encouragement Joss needs. She pulls out an Uno Robo-Attack, the old-fashioned card game jazzed up with a little robot that shoots out cards when you least expect it. I've played it a few times at friends' houses, though all we have at home is the original game.

"I thought you were crazy when you gave me this last Christmas," Myrlie says, pepping up a little. "But it's actually a pretty fun game."

After a few rounds, all three of us are much more energized, throwing down the "Hit Four, Robo-Scum!" cards with great relish. Myrlie is even laughing again.

"When I was a little girl, my great-aunt Agatha would have been scandalized by the notion of playing cards on Sunday," she says. "And with a minister, no less!"

"Your great-aunt Agatha obviously had no sense of humor," Joss says. "And no appreciation for the importance of playfulness in God's world."

She hits the button on the top of the Attack Robot and groans when it spits six cards at her.

"Appreciate playfulness, remember?" Myrlie taunts her. She frowns at her own handful of cards. "Sorry, Bethany, this is the only green card I have."

She puts down a "Zap! Hit-fire!" card, which usually would mean that I'm at the mercy of the Attack Robot, too.

"Oh, don't be sorry," I say. "Save your pity for . . . yourself!" I lay down my "Throwback Attack" card, which makes her, not me, the robot's victim.

"Great play!" Joss crows. She throws her arm around my shoulder, as if the two of us are ganging up on Myrlie. "Oh, Elizabeth," she says, "it's so nice having you back! I've missed . . ."—she gets a stricken look on her face—"you," she finishes lamely.

All three of us freeze. The Attack Robot's eyes flash red and green and yellow, like some malfunctioning traffic signal. *Stop, go, caution . . .*

"I wish we could pretend I didn't say that," Joss says quietly. "I know you're not Elizabeth. I'm sorry."

The Attack Robot hums at us. Joss and Myrlie stare at me, their expressions mirroring one another: mixtures of regret and compassion and confusion and fear.

"Am I really that much like her?" I ask forlornly.

"Yes . . . no . . . ," Myrlie says, at the same time that Joss says,

"No . . . yes." They look at each other and shrug.

"You saw the video," Myrlie says apologetically. "There is a strong resemblance."

"It's like, you know how things look different when you look at them out of the corner of your eye, instead of straight on?" Joss says. "Out of the corner of my eye, you *are* Elizabeth. Same features, same expressions, same person. But straight on, you're different."

"You're a lot quieter than Elizabeth," Myrlie says. "More . . . self-contained."

"Elizabeth could be such a spaz," Joss says. "Hyperkinetic. And so sure of herself—'I'm going to be in the Olympics, I'm going to win more gold medals than anyone else, I'm going to be the most famous gymnast ever.'"

"She was ambitious," Myrlie agrees. "Hillary was like that too, as a child. And then when Elizabeth was born, she transferred all her ambition to her daughter. . . ."

She glances toward me as if she wonders if she should have said that. I am also Hillary's daughter.

I think back to the years before my mother cried full-time. Was my mother ambitious for me?

Oh, honey, don't worry about it. You're doing the best you can, she'd tell me when I was little and I couldn't quite manage to color inside the lines.

You don't need those friends. You've got Mommy and Daddy, she'd tell me in third, fourth, fifth grade when I fretted about my ranking in the various popularity contests of school.

Let's just stay home together, she'd say when I suggested going just about anywhere: the skating rink, the zoo, a play. If I pushed at all, she'd give in. But I had to push.

My mother isn't ambitious for me, I think. *She's done every-thing she can to hold me back.*

I shove myself away from the table and the Uno Attack Robot and Myrlie and Joss.

"I don't want to play anymore," I say, sounding just like a spoiled little kid. "I'm tired. I'm going to bed."

"That's fine, dear," Myrlie says.

"I'll see you tomorrow," Joss says. "Good night."

They watch me climb the stairs. I know they will talk about me after they think I'm in bed, out of earshot. I am tempted to creep back down to the landing, press my ear against a wall and listen, out of sight.

Instead I pull my pillow over my head and clutch it tightly to my ears, so there's no danger of any sound leaking in.

—TWENTY·TWO—

When I wake up the next morning, I find Joss puttering around in the kitchen. But Myrlie is missing.

"She went on in to work, since I'd be here with you today," Joss says casually. "She's got one kid in her class she's really worried about—she didn't think he'd do well, having another day with a sub. You don't mind, do you?"

I know I'm supposed to say, "No, that's all right. It doesn't matter." I'm supposed to remember that Myrlie had a life before I showed up on her doorstep, that she's responsible for an entire classroom of kindergarteners. She's not actually supposed to be responsible for me. My parents are. And it's not like she's left me alone. Joss is a perfectly acceptable substitute. She's an adult too, however much she may clown around. She's a minister, for God's sake.

Still, I want to say, childishly, "I *do* mind. Make her come home. *Now*."

If that kind of strategy worked, I would have gotten Mom and Dad back, I'd be home in Pennsylvania, I'd know the answers to all the questions I've wanted to ask ever since I arrived in Illinois.

I grunt noncommittally and reach into the cereal cupboard.

"I had some of the leftover chocolate cake for breakfast, myself," Joss says. "I know Mom and Aunt Hillary would be horrified, but, hey, they're not here. Want some?"

"No, thanks," I say. I notice a box of instant oatmeal beyond the cereal. I grab it instead. Moments later, I've just taken my first bite when I realize Joss is staring at me. I lower my spoon.

"Elizabeth loved oatmeal, too, didn't she?" I say miserably. Myrlie's exact words ring belatedly in my head: *She'd choose it over chocolate.* And now that's just what I've done.

Joss nods slowly.

"What do you say we put a moratorium on Elizabeth talk today?" she says. "Pretend she never existed?"

"Sounds good to me," I say.

"That is, unless *you* want to bring her up, as a topic of conversation," Joss says. She hesitates. "What do you think about your parents? Do you want to make them off-limits too?"

I think about this. Joss knew my parents twenty years ago, when they were Walter and Hillary Krull, so she might be able to provide some insight I don't have. But Walter and Hillary Krull were Elizabeth's parents, not mine.

"They're *verboten* too," I say. For a second I think Joss might want to comment on my choice of words, maybe mention that *verboten* was one of Elizabeth's favorites too. But Joss only shrugs.

"Fine by me," she says. "Any other ground rules you think we ought to have?"

We discuss all sorts of restrictions, even ridiculous ones, like banning any mention of SpongeBob SquarePants. I can see what Joss is doing, trying to make me feel like I have some sort of power, some small sense of control. But seeing through her ploy doesn't make it any less effective. I can't summon my parents back, I can't make the phone ring, I can't understand why my last name is Cole when my sister's last name was Krull. But I find a tiny glimmer of happiness voting thumbs down on SpongeBob.

"Okay, so we know what we can and can't talk about," Joss says. "What are we going to *do* today? Mom says you're big on swimming—"

"I don't want to do that today," I say quickly.

"Fine, fine," Joss says. "It'd be crazy to stay indoors today anyhow. According to the radio, today is supposed to be absolutely stunning, autumn's last gasp of glory before we all *fall* into winter—no pun intended, of course. And it just so happens there's an incredible park just twenty minutes from Sanderfield. . . ."

So we go hiking. McCutcheon State Park, I discover, is a beautiful near-wilderness with windy trails that stretch my leg muscles every bit as much as a swim session would have. I'm tempted to ask Joss what kind of memories she has of this place—were there family picnics here back in the seventies and eighties and nineties? Did Elizabeth hang upside down from that tree over there? Did either of the girls fall down and scrape their knees on that rock over here? But I stifle those questions and pretend that Joss and I are both discovering the park for the very first time.

Joss proves to be a good guide, full of information about why different trees turn different colors, which kind of tree will lose its leaves first. As we near a clearing on our trail, she dives down and grabs a small, fanlike yellow leaf.

"Ginkgo," she says, and looks around. "Aha."

She points at a brilliant yellow tree off to the side, beautifully shaped, its branches gracefully swaying in the breeze.

"Imported from China," she says. "I don't know what it's doing here. Ginkgo is a prehistoric species. They've survived for centuries, even though most of the other plant life from their time period went extinct a long time ago. And scientists consider them absolutely unique, in a class by themselves, because they can't really be classified as either conifers or deciduous."

"How do you know so much about trees?" I ask.

"I was a double major in college," Joss says. "Religious studies and biology."

I give her a dubious look, and Joss laughs.

"I know," Joss says. "Both of my advisers thought I was absolutely crazy."

I pick up a handful of ginkgo leaves and arrange them all stemside down, like a bouquet. Then I release them into the wind.

"Didn't that get confusing, taking tests?" I ask. "Did you have to keep reminding yourself which class you were in? You know, that whole thing about creationism and evolution . . . ?"

"I didn't get confused at all," Joss says. "Science and religion deal with different questions. Science is *how* things happen and religion is *why*. The problem comes when people forget what they're asking of whom. Now, when do you think we should stop for lunch?"

"What category does that question fit in?" I ask. "Science or religion?"

"Now you're really taxing my mind, you little smart aleck," Joss says, and playfully swings her backpack at me.

When we arrive back at Myrlie's house, hours later, I feel like I'm returning from a vacation. I've got windburned cheeks and a

slightly sunburned nose. My calf muscles have that same pleasant little ache that I get after swimming. And I've mostly managed
to avoid thinking about Elizabeth or my parents the entire day.

But then as we're walking across the porch I notice the
empty hooks on the ceiling where the swing once hung—the
swing where Elizabeth and Joss sat, all those years ago. And
when we walk in the front door, Myrlie is there on the couch,
huddled over papers strewn across the coffee table. She starts
to gather the papers together when she sees us, then gives up
and just leans back against the couch.

"What's all this?" Joss asks.

"I got a package from Walter, today," Myrlie says. "We don't have
to worry about emergency medical care for Bethany anymore."

I pick up a paper from the edge of the table. It's a form written in hard-to-follow legal terms, but it seems to be giving Myrlie the right to take care of me in any circumstance, in
whatever way she thinks is best. It's signed in my father's familiar handwriting, "Walter Cole."

"See?" I say, holding it up. "Didn't I tell you—?"

But I look over, and Joss is holding a similar form. It's signed
"Walter Krull."

I reach down and there are more papers, signed "Walter
Ebern," "Walter Stanton," even "Walter Ronkowski."

"He sent your birth certificate, too," Myrlie says. "Certificates, I mean."

According to the papers in front of me, I am Bethany Cole,
born in Riverview, Pennsylvania; or Bethany Ebern, born in Albu-
querque, New Mexico; or Bethany Stanton, born in Viewmont,
Minnesota; or Bethany Ronkowski, born in Atlanta, Georgia.

"He wrote that I should keep all of these safe," Myrlie says, holding up a scrawled note. "Only use them if I have to. What did he think I was planning to do?"

Joss and Myrlie stare at me, like they think I might have an answer, like they think I might know more than I've told them.

"Who am I supposed to be?" I whimper. "Who am I *really?*"

No one answers.

"Let me see the envelope," Joss says. "Where was he when he mailed this?" She hunts through the papers and surfaces with a padded cardboard mailer. But there's no return address. The only postmark says "Sanderfield, Illinois."

"He could have tossed this in a mailbox Thursday night as he left town," Myrlie says in disgust.

"Or he could be hanging out just a few miles down the road," Joss says. "Ever think of that?"

"I've thought of a lot of things," Myrlie growls. "The next time Walter calls, I have a million questions for him."

Joss is still examining the envelope. She peers down into it, then looks up, her expression more troubled than ever.

"Um, Mom, did you see this?" she asks.

"What?" Myrlie asks, distracted.

Joss reaches into the envelope and pulls out something wrapped in more paper. This paper, though, only reads, "In case Bethany needs anything."

Joss pulls the paper off, revealing two thick wads of more paper. Cash.

Hundred-dollar bills.

—TWENTY·THREE—

Joss reacts as if she's suddenly discovered a poisonous snake in her hand. She gasps and drops the money.

We all stare at the two bundles of money on the floor for a few moments, then Myrlie bends over and picks them up.

"One, two, three . . . ," she mutters, counting the bills without breaking the paper bands holding them together. Joss and I do nothing but watch her until she finally finishes and announces, "There's ten thousand dollars here."

Joss and I still don't say anything.

All the money has that crisp, new look to it that you see in movies, when kidnappers demand suitcases full of cash, or when drug dealers buy off someone's silence. My own father sent that money to Myrlie, and I'm still thinking, *This can't be legal. Did he steal it? Did he kill someone for this money?*

"Why would Uncle Walter send that amount of money

through the *mail?*" Joss asks, finally breaking the silence. "Why didn't he just hand it to you Thursday night, in person?"

Myrlie shrugs helplessly. "What am I supposed to do now?" she asks.

Then they both seem to remember that I'm standing right there, that it's my father who baffles them, that the money is, I guess, technically mine. Myrlie gathers all the papers into a neat stack and places the two bundles of cash on top.

"I'm sure there a perfectly, uh, *rational* explanation for all this," she says. "It's a little hard to understand right now, but surely, when your father tells me what's going on, everything will make sense."

Myrlie is trying so hard, it makes me want to cry.

"Mom," Joss says. She darts her eyes toward me, then away. "You've got to consider all the possibilities. Uncle Walter sent you forged documents." Myrlie starts to object, but Joss persists. "You know at least three of the birth certificates are false, because how could Bethany be four people at once? So there's forgery. That's a crime. And he sends you this huge sum of money, through the mail, uninsured. That's pretty suspicious, don't you think? What if you're arrested for receiving stolen goods? What if opening that package makes you an accomplice?"

Myrlie's shaking her head, refusing to accept Joss's version.

"No," she says. "Walter's not a criminal. He wouldn't do anything like that."

"You don't know Walter anymore," Joss says. "You've barely seen him in twenty years."

It's been just four days since I saw my father, but I feel like he's become a stranger to me, too. Evidently he's always been a stranger, keeping secrets I can't begin to comprehend.

"He's gone crazy," I whisper. Is it better to believe my father's insane than that he's committed a crime? It's like that board game, Dilemmas, where you have to choose between two bad alternatives. *Would you rather be blind or deaf? If you were executed, would you choose lethal injection or the electric chair?* I'm not very good at Dilemmas, because my answer is always, "Neither. I want a different choice." I don't want my father to be crazy or a criminal.

Myrlie sighs heavily.

"You think I should go to the police, don't you?" she says.

Joss frowns apologetically at me, then nods.

"Not until I've had a chance to talk to Walter," Myrlie says. "I want to hear his explanation first."

I'm amazed at Myrlie's sense of loyalty.

Does my father deserve it? I wonder, as my head spins with questions. *Or does he deserve to be caught, to be punished, to be sent to jail?*

I can't think of any punishment for my father that doesn't also punish me.

"You didn't see Walter that night," Myrlie is telling Joss. "When he dropped off Bethany. He looked so . . ." She glances at me as she searches for the right word.

Go ahead. Say it, I think. *Tortured. Tormented. Distraught. Even—*

"Pitiful," Myrlie finishes. "He's a broken man."

It's all I can do not to gasp. "Pitiful" is so much worse than anything I expected her to say. The word seems to burrow under my skin, to sting at my eyes. I can't look at Myrlie or Joss. I can't look at the stack of documents and the money. I can't let myself think about who I am or what my parents might have done.

I am pitiful too.

—TWENTY·FOUR—

Myrlie hides the entire package in a fire-safe box at the back of one of her closets.

My father doesn't call.

The three of us eat dinner, and Joss begins to make noises about how she really should be getting back to St. Louis.

My father doesn't call, and Joss doesn't leave.

The hour hand on Myrlie's kitchen clock swings past seven, then eight, then nine, and Joss and Myrlie debate possible plans for me for the next day. Should Myrlie take another day off work? Should I be left home alone? Should I be enrolled in Sanderfield Middle School using one of the birth certificates Dad sent us? (And if so, which one?) Should I go to work with Myrlie? Should I maybe even go to St. Louis with Joss?

I listen to the conversation ping-ponging back and forth between Myrlie and Joss as if they're talking about somebody else's fate. Bethany Ronkowski's, maybe? Bethany Stanton's? I think that I really ought to tell Myrlie what my dad said about school and about it not being safe to leave me alone, but I'm mad at him now, getting madder by the minute. He abandoned me and he's probably a criminal and I don't care if I ever see or talk to him again.

The phone rings.

All three of us jump for it, but Myrlie reaches it first. Joss and I crowd in close, and I get a ridiculous image in my head of giggly girls at a sleepover, huddled together over a single phone crank-calling someone's boyfriend. I've heard that those things happen, late at night, after I've had to leave.

"Hello?" Myrlie says.

I hear my mother's voice coming through the receiver, sounding surprised: "Why, hello, Myrlie, I didn't expect you to be there. Could I speak to Elizabeth, please?"

Myrlie winces, but somehow manages to keep her voice steady.

"No, Hillary, Elizabeth isn't available right now. Could you put Walter on? I really need to talk to him."

"Sorry, Myrlie, I can't do that. Walter doesn't even know I'm calling." Mom lowers her voice confidentially. I can barely hear. "I'm not supposed to call, you know. I just wanted to talk to Elizabeth. . . ." Her voice trails off, like she's about to hang up.

I grab the phone out of Myrlie's hand.

"Hi, Mom," I say.

"Oh, *Elizabeth*, I'm so happy you could get to the phone," she says. "Isn't it nice that Myrlie could come and visit you in the hospital? Myrlie always loved you so—everyone loves you, you're such a wonderful girl. I'm so sorry about what happened. I didn't see that truck coming—I didn't! And he didn't see me. . . . Why weren't the signs clearer? Oh, my poor, poor baby girl . . ."

"Mom, it's okay. It's not your fault," I say uncomfortably. I don't want to keep impersonating Elizabeth, but I'm scared Mom will hang up if I say anything that brings her back to the present.

Joss slides a note to me that says, "Keep her talking! I'll have this call traced." Out of the corner of my eye, I can see her searching through her purse, pulling out a cell phone.

"I don't have access to stuff like that on my phone," Myrlie hisses at Joss, and Joss shakes her head frantically and hisses back, "It doesn't matter—in an emergency I'm sure there's a way. . . ." Part of me is listening to them and thinking, *Is this an emergency?* and, *I wish we'd known to trace Dad's call that first day.* But mostly I am straining to hear my mother's breathing, straining to make sure she's still there.

"Everything's okay, Mom," I repeat into the receiver, but my voice comes out sounding timid and scared.

"Honey, you don't have to try to be brave for me," Mom says. "I know you're in a lot of pain, and the doctors say the end isn't far away. But, listen, don't worry. Walter says . . . your father says . . ."

I see Myrlie's finger inch forward, poised to press a button on the phone's base. "Don't cut her off now!" I want to scream, but I can't get the words out. I see the three small letters above the button Myrlie's pushing: REC. Myrlie's not ending this conversation. She's recording it.

"Your father says we can get you back," Mom says. "If we save some of your cells, it'll be like you never died."

"I don't understand," I say. I'm gripping the phone so tightly my fingers are numb. I've lost all sense of feeling in my hand.

"Oh, Elizabeth, it's simple. Simple and fabulous." My mother's voice reverberates with joy now, all her sorrow washed away. "We'll make a copy of you."

"A . . . copy?" I repeat stupidly.

"Yes," my mother says. "There's another name for it. We'll have an exact copy. A clone."

I drop the phone. I've never fainted before, but that's what I do now, plunging straight toward the floor. Straight down.

—TWENTY·FIVE—

I fight my way back toward consciousness through an awful darkness and a throbbing pain in my head.

"—seriously injured?" Joss is saying.

"I don't think so," Myrlie says. My hearing goes in and out, so I only catch part of her next words: "... in shock ..."

I have to get back to the phone, have to get my mother to take back those words she just said. *You did not copy Elizabeth. You didn't. You couldn't.* I manage to raise my head and reach my arm toward the phone, which is dangling by its twisty cord over the edge of the counter. But then I hear what's coming out of the phone: the empty, monotonous dial tone.

I drop my arm.

"What happened?" Myrlie says. She's hovering over me, her anxious face seeming to float above mine. Somehow I've ended up with my head in her lap. She is stroking the hair back from my face. "What did Hillary say?"

I open my mouth but can't speak. I probably look like a guppy.

Joss crosses the kitchen, presses a button on Myrlie's phone. My mother's voice spills out: "Your father says we can get you back. . . . Oh, Elizabeth . . . We'll make a copy of you. . . . A clone."

"It's not possible," I say, finding my voice at last.

But Joss and Myrlie are both looking down at me now, and their faces say everything: *Bethany looks exactly like Elizabeth, even down to the lopsided freckles on her cheeks. Bethany likes the same foods Elizabeth liked. Bethany's voice sounds like Elizabeth's. Could it be . . . ?*

I scramble away from my aunt and my cousin, moving backward on my arms and legs like a frantic crab. I crash into a cabinet.

"I'm not that much like her. She was a gymnast!" I yell. But I can hear my old gym teacher's voice echoing in my head, *You have a lot of natural ability. . . .* I sag against the cabinet door. "Is it possible?" I whimper.

Myrlie and I both look at Joss. Joss, the biology major.

"They cloned the first sheep in Scotland when I was still in college," she says slowly. "This wacko religious sect, the Raelians, claimed to have produced a human clone years ago. Everyone assumed that was a hoax. But maybe . . ."

"Walter went into medical research after the accident," Myrlie says.

Joss frowns.

"Oh, Mom, human cloning would have been such a long shot thirteen years ago. It'd be a long shot now, because there have been so many laws passed against it. There's no support for it. For Uncle Walter to have cloned Elizabeth, it would have taken years of research, meticulous attention to the DNA, millions of dollars. . . ."

She stops, and I can tell that she's thinking of those crisp one-hundred-dollar bills my father sent us.

"I'm not a clone!" I scream. "I'm a real person, not just some—some Xerox of Elizabeth. I'm Bethany! Bethany Cole!" Then I remember that "Cole" might very well be an alias. How real can I be if I'm not even sure of my last name? "She was lying!" I scream, more frantically now. "My mother's delusional!"

Joss and Myrlie stare at me. And I can tell from their faces that one of my favorite words—"delusional"—had been one of Elizabeth's favorites too.

I leap up and flee the kitchen, as if I can run away from everything Elizabeth was. As if I can run away from myself.

—TWENTY·SIX—

I fling myself out the front door of Myrlie's house, across the porch, down the stairs, out the gate. I am running blindly, stumbling over my feet, falling, scrambling back up. I'm not watching where I'm going. I find myself in the middle of the street, but it doesn't matter, the only car lights are a block away. I dash back onto a sidewalk, force myself to pay enough attention to stay on concrete, not asphalt.

My body takes over, working into a rhythm as natural as swimming. Running is not my sport, but I can do it without thinking, my feet pushing against the pavement, my arms pumping hard.

I like to run and paint and read and watch TV and go to movies, Elizabeth had said on the videotape. Running was something else that belonged to her, then.

Half-panting, half-crying, I slow to a fast walk. But walking is a mistake, because it makes it easier to think.

Where am I going?

I'm in a strange town and it's dark and I'm lost now. Even if I wanted to, I couldn't find my way back to Myrlie's. And I don't want to go back to Myrlie's; I want to go back to Green-leaf, Pennsylvania, back to my old life, back to six months ago when Mom didn't cry (mostly) and Dad acted normal (mostly) and I didn't know anything about Elizabeth.

It's not possible . . .

I look around, searching for some recognizable house or street sign. But the houses are dark, the street signs covered in shadow. I can't even see the moon or stars, just dark clouds pressing low, crowding down against the treetops. I have never before been outside by myself after dark, certainly not lost in a strange place like this, not when I'm already bewildered and distraught. I have no hope of navigating my own way to safety.

I hear footsteps behind me, and it makes me think of all those things my parents have always feared for me. Young girls kidnapped from a dark street, young girls killed or left for dead . . . I take off running again, speeding through the darkness. My leg muscles cramp and burn; my breathing comes out ragged. I can't run forever. Eventually I'll have to stop; eventually I'll be caught.

Someone is shouting behind me: "Wait!"

I trip and sprawl across the ground, a searing pain in my leg.

"Bethany?"

It's Joss. She's running toward me, breathing hard.

"Are . . . you . . . okay?" she pants.

I stop struggling to scramble back up. It feels good to give up, to lie still. Joss collapses on the ground beside me.

"I was lost," I blubber. "I didn't know where I was."

"Town . . . square . . . now," Joss says, still trying to catch her breath. "We were about ten blocks away when you started that sprint. Man, I'm feeling old."

I roll over and sit up. We are on the courthouse lawn; I just barely missed falling into those chrysanthemums that Myrlie was so proud of planting. What I tripped on, I realize, was one of the steps leading to the memorial to Thomas Wilker.

"I thought I heard someone," I say. "Chasing me."

"It was probably just *me*," Joss says. "I didn't want you wandering around in the dark all by yourself."

Her face glows with concern, and in spite of myself I'm glad that she followed me. But I keep replaying those footsteps in my mind and they sound too heavy, too big, too ominous to belong to Joss.

"Anyhow, you're safe now," Joss says. She reaches over and brushes the hair out of my face. She peers at me, her eyes brimming with sympathy.

But is that sympathy really for me?

Who do you see when you look at me? I want to ask her. *Me, Bethany? Or Elizabeth, magically brought back from the grave?*

I remember what Joss said by accident, only the night before: *Oh, Elizabeth, it's so nice having you back!* Is that how my parents felt, every time they smiled at me, every time they kissed my forehead, every time they hugged me? Did they ever love me just as me?

I look around at the town square shops, dark and quiet and dead again. This time I don't think of hibernation; I think of the villagers in "Sleeping Beauty," who went to sleep for a hundred years while their princess slumbered. My brain shies away from the scientific implications of what my mother said, all that talk of cells and clones and DNA. But I can see my parents believing in something like the fairy tale ending, their beloved daughter magically revived.

Their *other* beloved daughter.

"It can't be true, can it?" I ask Joss. "What my mother said . . . Tell me she was lying. Tell me. Tell me."

I'm begging now, as if Joss has the power to change lies into truth, truth into lies. But Joss is shaking her head.

"I can't tell you that," she says. "I don't know if it's true or not."

"Oh, right," I say. "You don't know answers, just questions." I choke out a bitter laugh. "Hey, guess what? I bet this is one question you didn't ask when you were thirteen."

"Bethany . . . ," Joss begins, but I can't listen to her right now.

In the dim light, I look down at the palms of my hands, raw and red and scraped from my fall on the concrete. *My* hands, I say, but are they mine? Or are they Elizabeth's, revived, recycled, restored? Can I not even claim my own body as mine?

This is ironic: I'm terrible at sharing, everyone knows that, and now I'm expected to share not just my parents but my very *self* with some dead girl? I remember when I was five and Gretchen Dunlap from across the street just wanted to touch my Cabbage Patch doll. . . .

My Cabbage Patch doll, I think. *Oh, no.* Revelation is breaking over me, and it's horrifying. I clutch Joss's arm, and cut off whatever she was starting to say.

"They gave me Elizabeth's toys," I say weakly. I've just realized this. My Cabbage Patch dolls and *My Little Pony* videos and my original, unenhanced Uno game hadn't been antiques, lovingly reclaimed from the past just for me. They'd been Elizabeth's. Yesterday, I'd creeped myself out thinking about

Elizabeth's possessions boxed up in *my* basement or *my* attic, just a floor away from me. But they hadn't been boxed up and stored away. They'd been in my hands. I'd cradled her dolls in my arms when I was little, I'd snuggled up in bed with her stuffed animals practically every single night of my life.

"Lots of kids get hand-me-downs," Joss says mildly, trying to sound casual. "I had a friend in college who was the youngest of nine. She didn't own anything that hadn't belonged to one of her other siblings first."

"But your friend *knew* that," I say. "She knew what she was getting. She knew she wasn't the . . . the original owner." That word, "original," hangs in the air. I have to make myself talk past it. "I didn't know anything about Elizabeth," I say.

I think about the elaborate way Mom and Dad presented me with my collection of antique toys: the first Cabbage Patch doll arriving on my fifth birthday, the Uno game that same Christmas. I think about Mom saying they wanted an "exact copy" of Elizabeth; I think about my science teacher saying people are shaped by their environment as well as their genes.

"Oh, no," I moan. "Were they using the toys to try to make me just like Elizabeth?"

Joss is hugging me tight now; it feels like she's holding me together.

"They didn't make you take gymnastics lessons, did they?" she asks.

They didn't. In fact, they refused to let me become a gymnast. I hold on to that. But gymnastics was something Elizabeth had that I didn't—it's not much of a consolation.

"Was she . . . Did Elizabeth . . . ," I can barely get the words out. "Did she like to swim?"

Joss blinks down at me.

"No," she says. "Elizabeth hated swimming."

Relief floods over me. Here, finally, is something of mine that Elizabeth can't touch, can't ruin from beyond the grave. But the relief washes away quickly, leaving me still huddled in fear.

"Why?" I ask. "What's wrong with swimming?" I hate the way I've said that, as if whatever Elizabeth thought was the proper view. "What was wrong with her?" I say, a little too viciously.

Joss winces.

"Elizabeth almost drowned when she was really little," she says. "At the Sanderfield pool." Her voice slows down, as if she's straining to dive back into the memory. "Elizabeth got knocked down or shoved under—no one was ever quite sure how it happened. But then she was underwater and trying to breathe, and no matter how hard she tried to pull in air, she couldn't; she could only choke. Elizabeth could make such a scary story out of it. I can remember Elizabeth telling that story at sleepovers and around the campfire at gymnastics camp."

"Did they have to give her artificial respiration?" I ask. "The lifeguards? Or . . . Mom?" Somehow I can't imagine Mom responding very well in an emergency like that.

"Oh, no," Joss says. "It never got to that. Later on, Mom and Aunt Hillary always said Elizabeth exaggerated the whole story, that she couldn't have been underwater for more than a second or two. But Elizabeth refused to put her face in the water after that. Every year Aunt Hillary signed her up for swimming lessons, and every year Elizabeth stood on the side of the pool and wouldn't even dip her toe in. And then we got into gymnastics and Aunt Hillary stopped trying to make Elizabeth swim."

"Did *you* learn to swim?" I ask.

"Not until after Elizabeth died," Joss says. "Don't take this the wrong way, but swimming was kind of my declaration of independence from Elizabeth memories."

It can be mine, too, I think. *I swim, and Elizabeth didn't. There's no way I'm her clone.*

Then I remember how I fell in love with swimming after accidentally slipping into the water when I was three. I remember my parents' amazement that I liked being underwater, that I begged to go under again.

Were they trying to reenact Elizabeth's experience? They expected me to hate it, to panic, to be like Elizabeth and never step foot in the water again. But . . . I took a breath before I went down. Was that the only difference? Could Elizabeth and I have the same genes, but she hated swimming and I loved it just because I'd had the sense to take a quick breath when I was three?

And my parents let me be different, I think.

Somehow this makes me feel good, that my parents hadn't pushed my head back underwater until I choked, forcing me to be exactly like Elizabeth. But what kind of parents *would* do that, half-drown their child on purpose?

I shiver in the night air, the sweat from my panicky run finally drying off. For the first time I realize that I left Myrlie's house without so much as a jacket. My Greenleaf Swim Club T-shirt has long sleeves but it's lightweight, virtually no protection against the autumn breeze.

"We should be getting back," Joss says. "Mom will be worried to death about us."

She stands up, groaning about her stiff, sore muscles. I try to stand too, but my leg throbs and I fall again.

"I hurt my leg," I say. "I'm not sure I can walk on it."

"Let me see," Joss says.

She crouches down and tries to roll up the leg of my blue jeans. But the jeans are caked with blood.

"Ow!" I moan.

"Sorry," Joss mutters.

I turn my head and see a black car turn the corner and drive slowly—no, *crawl*—down the street between us and the row of dark shops. It's the first traffic I've seen in this silent, dead town square the whole time Joss and I have been sitting here. I'm puzzled: Did I hear the car coming from far off in the distance? Or was it sitting over on the other side of the courthouse the whole time? Did it just now start up and start rolling toward us?

I can't be sure.

The car pulls to a stop in front of us, angled across four empty parking spaces. The passenger side window slowly slides down.

"Is everything all right, Joss?" a man's voice calls out from deep inside the car. "Anything I can do to help?"

Joss turns around and squints toward the car. The man's face is totally in shadows.

"I'm sorry . . . do I know you?" she asks. "It's been a long time since I've lived in Sanderfield, and—"

"No reason you should remember me," the man says. But he doesn't tell her his name; he doesn't lean forward into the light. "Need a ride? It looks like Bethany banged up her leg pretty badly."

At least this guy didn't mistake me for Elizabeth, I think, feeling so relieved that I forget about the pain in my leg for a moment. But then I wonder, *How does he know my name?*

"Um . . . ," Joss says. She's looking back and forth between me and the man in the car. I can tell she's debating whether it's safe to go with him, whether she can get me back to Myrlie's house without him.

Another car turns the corner, much more quickly than the first. It toots a sort of siren-horn, then pulls in at the proper angle in front of the other car.

This one's a police car.

"Looks like help has arrived and you don't need me," the man says. "Bye."

He rolls up the window, puts the car in reverse, and maneuvers out past the police car. He waves as he drives off.

How did you know my name? I want to scream after him. *Why did you drive off so quickly—were you scared of the police? HOW DID YOU KNOW MY NAME?*

Joss has turned her attention to the officer climbing out of the police car.

"Bridgie!" she calls out delightedly.

"That's Officer Ryan Bridgeman to you," the cop says.

"Aw, come on," Joss says. "I'm the one who caught you stealing cookies in kindergarten."

"And you convinced me to change my ways and turn away from my life of crime. Before I got in trouble with your mom." Officer Bridgeman glances over his shoulder, his eyes following the car that's driving away. He turns back to Joss. "We had several reports of someone running through town 'in obvious distress.' Those were Mrs. Wade's words; remember our old

English teacher? Is there anything I should be concerned about?"

I wait to see what Joss will tell him. She's the one who wanted to call the cops when my father sent all that money. Will she tell him the whole tangled story?

Will she tell him I'm a clone?

"I was just out jogging," I say, too loudly. "I tripped and hurt my leg." I lean forward, letting the hair hide my face because if Officer Bridgeman knew Joss in kindergarten, he probably knew Elizabeth, too. But I want so badly to look up at Joss to see if she's going to back up my story.

Oh, no, I think. *She's a minister. What if she's taken some oath to tell the truth, the whole truth and nothing but the truth at all times?*

At the risk of being recognized, I glance up quickly. Joss and Officer Bridgeman are staring at each other, and I sure hope they had some sort of romantic past together—maybe they were high school sweethearts, before one of them broke the other's heart. If not, they're spending way too much time looking at each other without talking.

"My cousin is quite the athlete when she's not injured," Joss says finally, a little faintly. "I'd ask you to give us a ride back to Mom's house, but then you'd probably have to fill out a lot of paperwork, justify the trip to taxpayers and the *Sanderfield Reporter.*"

"I've got to drive out that way, anyhow," Officer Bridgeman says. "So I can break it to Mrs. Wade that she's not the next Sherlock Holmes. I don't necessarily have to report in my paperwork that I have passengers."

I have the feeling that they've negotiated something I don't quite understand. Officer Bridgeman and Joss help me into the police car. I sit in the back, behind the screen that's supposed to separate the criminals from the cops. Joss sits up front.

"Did you know that other guy who stopped? In the black car?" Joss asks.

"No," Officer Bridgeman says. "That was a rental car from out of town. The plates weren't local, and there was a decal on the bumper. Why? He wasn't bothering you, was he?"

"Nooo . . . ," Joss says slowly. "He just offered to help."

I forget that my leg is throbbing because suddenly my head feels like it's going to explode. It's all I can do not to scream at Joss, right in front of the policeman, *But he knew our names! How did he know our names?*

—TWENTY·SEVEN—

Officer Bridgeman takes forever helping me into the house, saying hello to Myrlie, joking about how kindergarten taught him everything he knows, saying good-bye to Joss, and telling her to stop by the station sometime if she ever gets bored visiting Myrlie. The minute he finally leaves and Myrlie shuts the door behind him, I burst out, "How did he know our names?"

"Little Ry-Ry?" Myrlie says, looking confused. "Why, we've known the Bridgeman family since—"

"Not Bridgie," Joss says. "This other guy who drove up when we were sitting on the courthouse lawn."

Myrlie's eyes look troubled as she bustles around getting antiseptic and gauze and bandage tape for my leg. But her voice is calm as she tells Joss, "Oh, you remember what it's like living in Sanderfield. Everybody knows everybody else's business. How old was this guy? It was probably somebody who knew your father or even your grandfather, a billion years ago."

"Bridgie said he had an out-of-town rental car. And the guy didn't just know me. He knew Bethany," Joss says. "Mom, how many people even know that Bethany's here?"

"Everyone at school, because I had to explain why I took the day off on Friday. Mrs. Sells next door, because she saw Walter's car pull up Thursday night. And, of course, Ron Boesdorfer's mom and Tammy Sligo saw her at the Y," Myrlie says, distractedly. "Bethany, I'm sorry, but you're going to have to take those pants off before I can put this bandage on."

Embarrassed, I unfasten my jeans and ease them down. My T-shirt is long enough that it covers me practically down to my knees—I've stood in front of total strangers in less clothes than this, at swim meets. But I'm skittish after the conversation with my mom, the strange encounter in the town square. I'm half-afraid Myrlie and Joss will look at my knees and say, "Here's our proof. Elizabeth's kneecaps looked just like yours."

But Myrlie's preoccupied with dabbing antiseptic onto the gash above my ankle, and Joss is still interrogating her mother.

"How many of those people would remember Bethany's name?" Joss asks. "How many would tell it to some strange guy from out of town, who just happened to be in town square—an otherwise deserted town square, I might add—at ten o'clock on a Monday night when Bethany and I needed help?"

Myrlie eases a gauze strip over my wound.

"Joss, I think you may be blowing this out of proportion," she says quietly, cutting her eyes from Joss to me and back. "Walter never told me to keep Bethany's presence here *secret*."

I'm sure Joss can read Myrlie's expression as well as I can: It says, *Calm down. Don't upset Bethany. We can talk about all of this later.* I suddenly realize I've spent my whole life watching that same look pass between my parents.

"Joss isn't blowing anything out of proportion," I say. I swallow hard. I feel so naked and exposed in my underwear and T-shirt, in my body that might be an exact copy of Elizabeth's. But I'm not going to be left out of this conversation. "Were you able to trace my mother's call?"

Myrlie shakes her head.

"It turns out, if the phone company traces a call, they send the information to the police. So . . . I didn't do that." She won't meet my eyes. She's focused on pressing the bandage tape firmly across the gauze over my wound. Then she's done and she has to look up. "The lady at the phone company said I could do 'dialback,' for a one-time fee, without anyone else knowing about it. I tried that, but it just rang and rang and rang. . . . And then the lady took pity on me and told me your mom must have used one of those gas station cell phones."

Is Myrlie's news supposed to make me feel better? I remember a school assembly we had last year when some police officer came and talked about personal safety. He said there'd been a big campaign by some charity to put cell phones in ladies' rest rooms in all sorts of public places, like gas stations and malls.

"Runaways, abused women, kidnap victims—anyone can use those phones," the police officer said. "And no one can tell where you're calling from."

"Well, duh, if you're being kidnapped, wouldn't you want someone to know where you were?" one of the kids in my class yelled up to the stage.

"I mean, no one outside of law enforcement," the policeman

said, like we'd all been stupid not to figure that out.

Last year, I hadn't thought those phones would ever have anything to do with me. I wonder, suddenly, if my mother could be considered a runaway, an abused woman, or a kidnap victim. Or maybe all three?

"If we go to the police . . . ," I say slowly.

"Not yet," Myrlie says, avoiding my eyes again. "Let's sleep on it. All of us. Joss, I hope you weren't still thinking you'd drive back to St. Louis tonight. Is there any way you could wait until morning?"

"I'm not going back to St. Louis," Joss says. "I'll call the church tomorrow and tell them I need to take some time off. I'm staying right here."

She stares down fiercely at Myrlie and me, her dark hair flared out from her face like a helmet, the torn knee in her blue jeans hanging down like a badge of honor. I'm so glad that she's not leaving. But her announcement scares me too. If she is staying, that means she believes there's something to be afraid of. I feel like we are battening down the hatches, lifting the drawbridge, locking the shutters, preparing for some huge storm or battle or revelation. But I don't know what's coming. How can I understand what lies ahead of us when I don't even know who I am?

—TWENTY·EIGHT—

The wound on my leg wakes me in the night. It throbs, a pain and a reminder of pain. I sit up and click on the bedside light, then peel back the tape Myrlie used to seal the bandage. The gash on my leg is ugly and red and deep. Maybe I should have gotten stitches. Maybe Myrlie would have rushed me to the emergency room if it hadn't meant using one of those documents my father had sent. If it hadn't meant she had to decide which paper to use.

I'm going to have a scar, I think. *Mom and Dad won't like that.*

And then it seems silly to worry about a scar, a little puckered skin, when I have so many other problems.

At least it will be something different, I think. *Elizabeth didn't have a scar on her leg.*

If I cut my hair and dyed it, and got colored contacts, and pierced my eyebrow, and maybe carved a scar in my cheek, I wouldn't look like Elizabeth at all anymore. Nobody would mistake me for her.

But I wouldn't look like *me* anymore either.

I twist around in my bed, and my thoughts tangle as badly as my sheets and blankets. I don't know if I'm mad at Elizabeth for looking like me or at myself for looking like her; I don't know if I hate my parents or if I miss them; I don't know why I couldn't have been just an ordinary, normal kid with an ordinary, normal family, like everyone else.

I hear a murmur of low voices downstairs, and this makes me mad too. Myrlie and Joss must be talking in secret, deciding my fate while they think I'm safely tucked away in bed, sound asleep. They must think I'm a child, too naïve and innocent and stupid to hear all the facts.

Well, I'm not. . . .

I slide out of bed and creep over to my door. I limp a little, because of my leg, but I manage to open the door and slip down the hall without making a sound. I peek around the corner, down the stairs to the living room.

It's not Myrlie and Joss down there talking. It's just Joss, sitting in the dark with the TV on and the sound turned low.

I dare to ease down a few steps because I think if I lean out from the railing and crane my neck a little, I'll be able to see more than the ghostly glow of light in front of the TV. I'll be able to see what Joss is watching. But the second step down creaks. Joss stares up at me and gasps.

"E—" she starts to say, then chokes back the word. She swallows hard. "That stairs has always creaked," she says, her voice suddenly too glib. "Elizabeth and I made a game out of avoiding it whenever we spent the night with Grandma. We'd sneak around and pretend the grown-ups couldn't see us. . . ." She breaks off, then mutters, "Sorry."

I'm not sure if she's apologizing for talking about Elizabeth, or for not being able to cover up the fact that she started to call me the wrong name again.

I stand frozen, halfway up and halfway down the stairs.

"You couldn't sleep either, huh?" Joss asks softly.

"No," I say, and somehow her question frees me to continue climbing down the stairs.

I stop beside the couch, as soon as I can see the TV screen. It shows two girls, probably about eight years old, jumping on a trampoline. One is dark and one is blond—it's Joss and Elizabeth, Elizabeth and Joss. They're both screaming, "Look at this one! Look at me!" and then flinging themselves high into the air, spinning and whirling seemingly dozens of times before landing back on their feet.

The colors are so bright on the TV screen—so much more vivid than anything else in this dark room.

"I'll turn it off," Joss says quietly. She fumbles for the remote.

"No," I say, surprising myself. I'm steeling myself for something. Joss waits. "It was nice today, pretending Elizabeth didn't exist," I say, finally. "But I don't think . . . I don't think I can do that anymore."

"You're probably right," Joss says.

I ease down onto the couch beside her, facing the TV head-on. Together we watch the two little girls from another time defy gravity again and again and again. They hop off the trampoline and eat ice-cream cones, the ice cream melting and dripping and rolling down their chins. They giggle and lick ice cream from their fingers. The tape crackles and hisses and goes black momentarily. Then suddenly it's winter: The girls are outside playing in the snow, making snowmen, throwing snowballs. Moments later, they're opening Christmas presents, they're hunting for Easter eggs, they're back outside in the sunshine, jumping on the trampoline again.

"Didn't you ever do anything alone?" I ask Joss.

"Not much," Joss says huskily.

The tape spools deeper into the night and I feel like I'm falling deeper into the past. It's hypnotic, watching those girls, those happy, innocent, ignorant little girls. They grow up before my eyes, passing through stages of glasses, braces, short hair, long hair, oddball fashions. They don't seem quite real. I realize that if I'm really an exact copy of Elizabeth—if that's possible, if that's true—then it's the same two people sitting on the couch, watching, as the two little girls turning cartwheels on the screen. But Joss-in-real-life-right-now has a few gray hairs and the beginnings of wrinkles beside her eyes; I can't believe that that dark-haired little girl on the screen could ever grow up. And the more I watch of Elizabeth, the more I feel that she is not me; I am not her. She mugs for the camera, she sings offkey without a hint of self-consciousness, she leans in close to the lens and whispers, confidentially, "You know, you'll be able to sell this tape for *a lot* of money when I'm famous."

Joss has tears in her eyes.

"It was so hard to believe that *she* was the one who died," Joss says. "She was so vibrant, so alive."

I'm not vibrant, I think. For the umpteenth time, I hear my mother's words echoing in my head: *We'll have an exact copy.* But they didn't get that. In the videos, everything about Elizabeth sparkles. She was spunky and confident and outgoing and talkative. I'm quiet and dreamy, hiding behind my glasses, hiding underwater. Were my parents disappointed?

Is that why they left me behind at Myrlie's?

"Whenever Elizabeth and I talked about going to the Olympics," Joss says, "we always planned for her to win all the gold medals, and I would get all the silver. And I never questioned that, never thought that maybe I would deserve any gold myself. Never thought I could be number one, as long as Elizabeth was around. Isn't that strange?"

She's not asking me. She's asking the little girl dancing on the screen in front of us.

"Why didn't my parents make me do gymnastics?" I ask. "I mean, if Elizabeth was good enough for the Olympics, if I'm supposed to be her . . ." I can't quite bring myself to say the word. *Clone.*

Joss gives me a measuring look.

"I think I know why," she says.

She leans over and digs through a box on the floor—the entire box of all the old videotapes. She pulls out one and exchanges it for the tape in the VCR. She fast-forwards through snow scenes and an ice storm and what look to be the first tulips of spring. And then we seem to be in some sort of gymnasium, and dozens of girls in leotards parade by. I pick out Elizabeth—she's the tallest one. It's some sort of competition; in the background I can hear an announcer calling out names on a loudspeaker with the same sense of hushed anticipation as at a swim meet.

The camera pauses for a second, then focuses in on Elizabeth mounting a balance beam. Elizabeth rolls, twirls—and falls. Even in the shaky videotape, I can see the astonishment, the humiliation on Elizabeth's face. *My* face. Elizabeth climbs back on and bursts into a series of spins above the beam, her hands not even touching. And then she finishes the spins and reaches down, every muscle in her body seeming confident that that beam will be right beneath her, right where she always knew it would be. Her fingers connect and she twists her body around, ready to land on her feet. But her feet slip. She falls again, plunging to the mat below. The screen goes black.

"She grew so fast, her center of balance was off," Joss says quietly. "That was her last gymnastics meet. She'd done that routine a hundred times before that, perfectly. But . . . that was the competition."

I can see my parents wanting to spare me the pain of falling like that, after soaring. My parents still don't even think that I should use sharp knives, for fear that I might cut myself. I look down at my hands—my long-fingered, broad hands that used to be so tiny and delicate. Somehow I'd always expected to be tall someday. Even when I was the shortest kid in my class, year after year, I always knew that I'd eventually outgrow the others. I can even remember telling a bully in fourth grade, "You just wait till I get my growth. Then *you'll* be scared of *me.*"

A sickening realization creeps over me.

Of course I knew I'd grow tall. My parents told me. And they knew because of Elizabeth. I think about how much uncanny knowledge my parents had always seemed to have. When I was in second grade, my mother had simply announced one afternoon, "Time to get glasses." And she'd taken me to the eye doctor and, yes, it was true, I was beginning to slip into myopia.

"Were you referred by the school nurse after a screening?" the eye doctor asked.

"No, I just had a feeling," Mom said.

Of course she did. Of course. She'd also known when I'd lose my first tooth, when I'd need my first bra. Because of Elizabeth.

I'm sinking so far into the horror of this revelation, that I've lost track of what's showing on the TV. Then Joss gasps.

"I didn't remember them taping this," she moans.

I look up and the TV shows the two girls, not so little anymore, standing in full sunlight in front of an array of summer flowers.

"Are you going to have fun today?" someone—Joss's dad?—asks from behind the camera.

"Oh, yes," Elizabeth says, tossing her head so that her hair streams out behind her in the breeze. The sunlight catches the golden glints in her ponytail. "We're going to ride every roller coaster ten times."

"Make sure you check back in with us every two hours." This is my mother's voice, the familiar note of anxiety buried deep within. "Be careful."

"I can't watch this," Joss says. She clicks off the remote and the TV goes dark. So does the entire room. "That was Sinclair Mountain. The amusement park. That last day. Before . . ."

The accident, I think.

We sit in silence. I think of glib things to say: *Well, you know, that was twenty-some years ago. You should be over it by now. Or, You know she died. Watching the tape's not going to change anything.* But I don't speak. Slowly my eyes adjust to the darkness. There's a little bit of moonlight coming in the window. I can see Joss in silhouette, shaking her head.

"That day was special," she says, her voice almost a whisper. "Mom and Dad and Uncle Walter and Aunt Hillary let us roam around by ourselves some. We felt so grown-up. We had boys flirting with us—well, with Elizabeth, anyway. Elizabeth just glowed. I can't describe . . . It was like that was my first glimpse into this new world of being a teenager—a world that Elizabeth was entering first. We walked around checking out the cute boys and making fun of our parents for being too chicken to ride the roller coasters and we felt . . . invincible. I remember thinking I was really going to like being a teenager, being in that new world."

"Did you?" I ask. I have not thought much about what it will be like to be a teenager. For the last six months, the sound of my mother's crying seemed to have drowned out every other thought in my head.

Joss shakes her head more violently now.

"I was still in the hospital when I turned thirteen," she says. "I was in pain. I couldn't stop thinking about how I'd spent the last day of my father's life avoiding him, how I'd acted like I was being really generous, letting Elizabeth choose which seat she wanted in the minivan, driving home. And then that choice killed her. . . . I'd think things like, Maybe God goofed, and maybe I was the one who was supposed to die. Or, if it wasn't a mistake, why did God want Elizabeth and Daddy dead? I was a pretty death-obsessed teenager. All the boys were scared of me. Everyone was. I never got that charmed-teenager life."

I won't either, I think. In the dark, I practice tossing my head the way Elizabeth had in the video. But there's no sunlight streaming down on me, and the movement makes the back of my head hurt. I must have banged it against the kitchen cabinet when I was scooting away from Myrlie and Joss, horrified at the notion that I might be Elizabeth's clone.

"Why did God want Elizabeth and your father to die?" I ask, because I'm working on something like a geometry proof in my head. If God wanted Elizabeth dead twenty years ago, and if I'm just like Elizabeth, then is there something wrong with my being alive now? Were my parents defying God—did they think they were God?

"Questions like that are hopeless," Joss says. "You can drive yourself crazy trying to fathom God's will so simplistically, putting everything into neat little boxes and categories. I don't think He wanted anyone to die. But He let it happen because of free will, because we're not God's little robots, preprogrammed to live out our lives without getting to make any choices of our own."

"Is that what they taught you to say in theology school?" I ask.

"Yes, but it's also what I believe," Joss says.

"What did they teach you about cloning people? Did they say anything about parents creating little robots, preprogrammed to be exact copies of someone else? Did they?" My voice arcs up. I am being surly and nasty with Joss, and maybe it's all because I can't toss my hair over my shoulder as well as Elizabeth did.

"There was a class that was something like 'The Theology of Newer Reproductive Techniques,' but I never took it," Joss says, shrugging apologetically.

"But most people think cloning is wrong," I say, my voice still harsh and rude. "Not just ministers. That's why there are laws against it. That's why there's something wrong with me."

Joss twists around and turns on the light behind her. I blink in the sudden brightness.

"Bethany," she says. "I don't know what Uncle Walter and Aunt Hillary did to get you. I don't know how you were, uh, conceived. But none of it would be *your* fault."

I look away, but there's nothing safe to look at.

"Let me tell you a story," Joss says. "Years after the accident, I was at a science museum. They had this bizarre exhibit about speed and momentum, using the example of four teenagers in an out-of-control car running into a tree. Someone had figured out that teenagers one and two would die if the car hit the tree at X speed. Five miles faster, it would be teenagers one and three. Ten miles faster and a last-minute turn of the steering wheel, only teenager four died, the others lived. In scientific terms, it all seemed so random, and I stood there at that exhibit just sobbing, and I wanted to yell at Einstein for that little quote of his about how God doesn't play dice."

"*Einstein* said that?" I ask.

"Yeah, pretty weird, huh?" Joss says. "The thing is, when I got done crying, I walked away from that exhibit with this strange sense of peace, and I didn't have to ask anymore why Elizabeth died, why Daddy died, why I didn't. The new question I was obsessed with was, 'Okay, I lived—now what am I supposed to do with my life?'"

"So you became a minister," I say sulkily.

"Well, not immediately," Joss says. "But later, yes. I'd spent a lot of time asking questions, but that was the first time I started listening for answers."

She's looking at me like I'm supposed to jump up and down and say, *Oh, thank you for helping me understand! That solves everything!* But my parents are still missing, I've still got my mother's voice echoing in my head, telling me I'm an exact copy of a dead girl. And I'm still worried about how the man in the black car knew my name.

"What am *I* supposed to do?" I ask.

"Hold on," Joss says. "Have faith. Don't think that there's something wrong with you because of this."

That's easy for you to say, I want to snarl at Joss. *Your parents didn't clone you.* But Joss is sitting there talking to me at four in the morning. She didn't go back to St. Louis. She chased after me when I ran away.

"I want to look at the package from my father again," I say.

"Okay," Joss says.

She climbs the stairs, avoiding the creaky step, and comes back a few minutes later with the packet that she and Myrlie and I were so startled by. I pull the sheets of paper out of the envelope, one after the other. They are all so cold and official, the bureaucratic language, the computerized printouts of all the different birth certificates. Each certificate has me being born at the exact same time, on the exact same date. This makes me feel more like a copy than ever. Only my parents' signatures are different, the loop of my father's "*l*" reaching higher on one form than another, the line of my mother's "*r*"s sloping differently. I put the certificates in a row. A handwriting analyst would probably be able to figure out which form was signed first—which one is real. I can only stare at the familiar cursive, my eyes blurring with tears. I pull out the paper that was wrapped around the bundles of money because it holds even more words in my father's writing: "In case Bethany needs anything." The paper slips from my shaking hand to land upside down on the carpet. I bend down to retrieve it and gasp.

"Did you see the back of this?" I ask Joss, because I don't think I can trust my own eyes.

"No—I was too shocked by all the money. What is it?" Joss leans over too, and picks up the opposite corner of the page. Together we lift it toward the light. "Oh, my gosh," Josh says. "It's an entire letter. Uncle Walter gave us an explanation after all."

—TWENTY·NINE—

Joss and I smooth out the paper on the coffee table. She turns on another light. We both bend our heads low over the page. I don't know about Joss, but I'm almost giddy with excitement, so eager finally to have a lucid, rational explanation—an explanation from my father, not my mother.

Then I read the first paragraph.

He is chasing me. He is hunting me down.
Thought he would stay in prison.
I lied to him. Lots of lies.

There's a gap, then in bigger writing it says, "NO REGRETS!!!" The "No" is underlined six times.

Lies were the only way to get Bethany.
Bethany, Bethany, Bethany . . .

The way he's written my name, again and again, it's almost like a caress. Or a lullaby. I can't stand to look at my own name in his writing—I have to skip ahead.

> Naming her Elizabeth would have been too much like tempting fate. Surely you understand why we chose Bethany—from the Bible.

"What's my name got to do with the Bible?" I ask Joss.

"Um . . ." Joss tears her gaze away from the page. "Bethany is a place mentioned in the New Testament. Jesus had friends there. Mary and Martha and . . . Lazarus."

She's looking at me like this is supposed to mean something.

"Who are they?" I say. "My parents never took me to church. I don't know what they believed."

Joss sighs.

"Lazarus died and Jesus brought him back to life," she says. "In Bethany."

"Oh," I say. I look back down at the letter, but my eyes have blurred and I can't seem to make the loops and lines of ink into words. It doesn't matter. "So, did you know right away, as soon as you heard my name, that I was supposed to be Elizabeth reincarnated or resurrected or . . . or recycled?" I ask. "Am I so stupid that I've been walking around all my life telling people I was a clone—just by saying my name?"

"Lots of girls are named Bethany," Joss says gently. "It doesn't have to mean anything."

I look back at the letter.

we made a deal with the devil and now the devil is demanding his due.

So sorry, Myrlie. Didn't mean to hurt you again. We do regret that, hurting you.

Can't come back now. Even Thursday, still had hope.

No hope now. He's going to catch us. Can't lead him back to you and Bethany. Can't even call. Have to protect you and Bethany.

Be good to Bethany. Take care of her.

This money—not tainted. All legal. Was Elizabeth's college fund. Now Bethany's. Tell Bethany we love her.

The tears come back when I read that last line.

"Come back and tell me you love me in person," I mumble, because it's easier to stoke my anger than to keep feeling so sad.

Joss glances at me, but she doesn't say anything. She looks back at the paper, though she's got to be done reading it. Her gaze glides across the page again and again.

"It's not really a letter, is it?" she says finally. "It's more like notes he took for what he wanted to say in a letter."

"It's more like the ravings of a lunatic," I say. I point at the first sentences: *He's chasing me. He's hunting me down.* "Isn't that, like, classic paranoia?"

"What if someone really is chasing him?" Joss asks.

And then I can't hold on to my anger. I think about my

parents, so fragile, my mother crying, my father holding her up. I think about how they looked in the videotapes Joss and I have been watching. They didn't make many appearances, because the camera was almost always focused on the girls. The adults showed up mainly as a torso in the background, a gloved hand bringing out a scarf and a carrot nose for the girls' snowmen, a pair of arms placing a birthday cake full of candles in front of Elizabeth or Joss. But the few times that my parents' faces flashed across the screen, they looked so young and happy, so normal. I do not like to think of them being old and crazy now. Or worse—old and in danger.

I reach out with one finger and trace three words toward the bottom of the letter: *Can't come back.*

"Is this true?" I ask Joss. "What if he never comes back? What if I never see my parents again?"

"Mom would take care of you," Joss says. "You wouldn't be left alone."

Joss doesn't understand. I'm not asking what will happen to me if my parents never return. I'm asking what will happen to them.

—THIRTY—

I go back to bed and sleep for hours. It's long after noon when I open my eyes in Myrlie's frilly yellow room that she decorated for her nonexistent grandchildren. I have my days and nights mixed up now; I feel like a vampire, living counter to all natural rhythms, scorned and feared by normal society.

Would you rather be a vampire or a clone? That would be a good Dilemmas question, I think. I try to picture myself sprawled out on the floor at one of my friends' houses—Molly's or Emma's or Lucy's—tossing the dice, moving the little marker around the board, answering profound questions with little jokes. But my old life seems like an illusion now, no more real than a movie. I didn't know Molly or Emma or Lucy very well. I didn't live in Greenleaf long enough to make any really good friends. I didn't live anywhere long enough for that. I was just a cardboard cutout of a person, a background prop in other people's lives.

Except for my parents'. I was always important to them. Center stage, I thought.

I get out of bed and go down the stairs because I don't want to think about my parents. A yellow school bus is sliding past Myrlie's front windows. I watch it stop and discharge a half-dozen kids who look to be about my age. They are arriving home; while I was sleeping they went through an entire day of school, math and science and language arts, lunch and gym and chorus. I try to imagine myself sitting on that bus, just another ordinary Sanderfield kid coming home from another ordinary day. I used to think I had a good imagination, but I can't stretch it that far.

"Good morning," Joss says behind me. "Or . . . good afternoon, I should say." She's sitting at a desk by the stairs, hunched over a laptop computer. "Want something to eat?"

"No . . ." I sink into the couch. I feel groggy and disoriented. Food would probably help, but do I really want to be able to think clearly?

"I told Mom to go on in to work today, so she wouldn't just sit around fidgeting and worrying," Joss says. "She'll be home in a couple hours."

"What are *we* supposed to do to keep from sitting around fidgeting and worrying?" I ask.

"I've been doing computer searches trying to look up all your parents' different aliases," Joss says. "I haven't had much luck."

I go and stand by the computer so I can look over her shoulder. All she's found is property transfers, a string of names and the places we've lived.

"Looks like your dad's been 'Walter Cole' for the past nine years," Joss says.

I shrug, because this tells me nothing.

"What about his jobs?" I ask. "He's always worked. He managed money."

"I can't find any evidence of that," Joss says. "You want to try?"

She slides away from the computer to give me access to the keyboard. I use every search engine I can think of. I Google, I Yahoo, I Ask Jeeves. All the Walter Coles, Walter Eberns, Walter Stantons, and Walter Ronkowskis I come up with are clearly the wrong people.

Then I type in Walter Krull.

The computer hums, mulling over the name. Finally it gives me three promising matches.

Two are news stories about dangerous intersections in the state of Illinois. Joss and I skip over those quickly.

The third match is in a long report about a company called Digispur and somebody named Dalton Van Dyne. The name sounds familiar, but I can't quite place it until Joss says, "Wait a minute. Isn't that the embezzler, the guy who just got out of prison?"

Out of prison. Joss and I stare at each other, and I can tell she's remembered the same line I'm thinking about from my father's letter: *Thought he would stay in prison.*

Joss starts scrolling rapidly down through the story, passing screenfuls of information without a single mention of my father. I click on the search-find function, and the pages advance until my father's name glows green in front of us:

It was discovered that Van Dyne diverted much of the money through fictitious employees. A Canadian office supposedly staffed by Sandra Despre, Walter Krull, Antonio Perez and Michael Sciullo never existed, and neither did any of those people.

Joss sags back against the chair.

"It's just a coincidence," she says.

"What if it isn't?" I ask. "What if my dad really did have some connection to the Dalton Van Dyne guy? What if . . . ?"

I can't quite bring myself to say what I'm thinking. But I reach down and press the keys to start a new search. This time I type in, "Digispur" and "cloning."

I get a hundred and sixty-two hits. Joss leans forward as I call up the first one, which is titled "Digispur CEO Outspoken Foe of Cloning." It's about some other guy, Errol Schwartz, not Dalton Van Dyne. Schwartz must have taken over the company when Van Dyne went to prison. Still, words pop out at me: ". . . evil technology . . . soulless copies . . . immoral, unethical . . . preposterous hubris of mankind . . ."

"Bethany, sit down," Joss says, but her voice seems to come at me from miles and miles away. I'm swaying.

Joss takes me by my shoulders and gently pushes me over to the couch. I bury my face in my hands and listen to the pulse pounding in my ears. The next thing I know she's forcing something into my hand. A glass. A glass of orange juice.

"You don't need to read that right now," Joss says. "Not on an empty stomach."

My face is burning. I sip the orange juice and press the cool glass against my cheeks. *Evil . . . soulless . . . immoral . . . unethical . . .*

"You believe it, don't you?" I ask Joss. "You believe I really am a clone. That's why you don't want me to read that."

"I don't want you fainting and getting a cut on your head as bad as the one on your leg," Joss says. She reaches back and shuts down the computer. "Now. Let's get something for you to eat, and then let's get out of this house, get you some fresh air.

We can take another hike or I'll take you to the Y to swim or—"

"No," I say, shaking my head violently. I can't stand the thought of being where anyone might see me—anyone who might recognize me as a copy of Elizabeth. "I . . . I want to stay here in case my dad calls again. My dad or my mom. I know he said he wouldn't but . . . what if he does?"

"Bethany," Joss says gently. "What if he doesn't? What if you spend the rest of your life waiting in this house and he never calls?"

Never is a very long time, I think. And for some reason that reminds me of another line in my father's letter: *No hope now.*

Joss is watching me carefully. She probably had some training to deal with depressed people. She's probably working on some mental checklist in her mind to see how far gone I am: Refuses to eat—check; Refuses to leave house—check.

"I'll go in the backyard," I say. "I can get fresh air there."

"Okay," Joss says.

Half an hour later, after I've been fortified with a peanut butter and jelly sandwich and a glass of milk, as well as the rest of the orange juice, we prop open one of the windows so we can hear the phone—"just in case," I tell Joss. And then we step out the back door.

It's gotten colder overnight, and a sudden gust of wind whips my hair against my face. The wind also brings a stream of autumn leaves down from the trees; it looks as though the trees are crying.

"We could rake some of these leaves for Mom," Joss says. "Though, as I remember, it's usually a losing battle. If you don't want to, we could just walk around."

"I don't mind raking," I say.

Joss goes into the garage to get rakes, and I stomp my feet, trying to stay warm. This makes my leg throb again, but I ignore it. I make myself walk without limping toward the nearest tree, where I see a wooden sign half-hidden in the leaves at its base. I bend down and push the leaves away: The sign reads, "Hillary Elaine Easton, March 29, 1953."

I think of the memorial plaque for Thomas Wilker on the courthouse lawn and shiver. Maybe there is more that I don't understand. This isn't exactly like a tombstone, but what if . . . ?

"Oh, you found your mom's tree," Joss says behind me.

"Huh?" I say, trying not to act as spooked as I feel.

Joss rolls her eyes.

"It's a family tradition my grandparents were really into," she says, handing me a rake. "Every time a new baby was born into the family, they planted a tree. Your mom's is a box elder, my mom's is that oak over there, and Elizabeth and I got those maples back by the fence. Supposedly the trees planted by my great-great-grandparents for their children and grandchildren are still thriving back in Ohio, where they grew up."

I can't help myself: I drift back toward the fence, looking for other little signs. Elizabeth's tree, it turns out, is the big, dramatic red tree I'd noticed my first morning at Myrlie's house. I stand at the foot of the tree looking up. A scar on the trunk, just above eye level, catches my attention.

"I did that," Joss says softly beside me. "After Elizabeth died, I was so mad that she was dead and her stupid tree was still alive that I tried to chop it down."

I look up again, taking in the full sweep of the branches over my head.

"You didn't succeed," I say.

"Partly, I was too weak, after the accident. Partly, I didn't really want to kill it. And partly . . . well, life wins. In the end, life always wins."

I don't understand what she means. So what if the tree lived? Elizabeth didn't, and neither did Joss's dad.

I start raking leaves. It is a little strange raking under Elizabeth's tree, so I move over, toward the trees without signs. We fall into a rhythm, Joss and I, not really talking except to grunt, "Can you hold the bag for me?" and, "Steady now." In spite of myself I am enjoying the exercise, the fresh air, the chance to move my muscles and not worry about myself or my parents or what I read on the computer screen. I like not thinking. By the time Myrlie's car pulls into the driveway, Joss and I have cleared practically the entire backyard.

"Mom is going to be so happy when she sees what we've done," Joss says.

Myrlie gets out of the car and runs toward us—evidently she's really eager to tell us just how delighted she is. But when she gets close I can tell that her face is stretched tight with anxiety.

"Did you see this?" she demands, shaking something at Joss. It's a newspaper. A page pulls away in the wind and I catch a glimpse of the *Sanderfield Reporter* masthead.

"Mom, it's okay," Joss says. "I checked the police report, and Bridgie didn't mention our names, so you don't have to worry about any of the neighbors gossiping—"

"No, *this*," Myrlie says. She holds out a page for Joss to see. I creep up behind her and peer over her shoulder. There, in big, black type in a boxed-in ad, are eight words.

WALTER COLE,
I NEED TO TALK TO YOU.

—THIRTY·ONE—

"Maybe it's a prank," Joss says, unconvincingly. "Or just a coincidence? Is there some other Walter Cole who lives here? Someone whose last name really is 'Cole,' and it's not an alias?"

Joss had tried to argue that the mention of "Walter Krull" on the computer was a coincidence too. I look over at Myrlie, and her expression is skeptical.

"I think Nancy Patterson works in the advertising department at the *Reporter*," Myrlie says. "I'm going to call her."

Myrlie turns on her heel and stomps off toward the house, a woman on a mission.

Joss looks at me doubtfully.

"Think we should finish up here?" she asks. "We don't have much left."

In fact, the only patch of leaves left is under Elizabeth's tree.

"I'm getting a blister," I say. I hold up my hand for evidence. "And I want to hear what Myrlie finds out."

Joss's expression is a battle of emotions, as if she wants to protect me but doesn't know how.

"Okay," she finally says. Giving up.

Joss puts the rakes away and I head toward the house. When I reach the kitchen, Myrlie is already on the phone.

"That's all you can tell me?" she's saying. "No, no, I don't want you to lose your job . . . ."

Myrlie hangs up and sits for a minute staring at the phone.

"Nancy can't tell me anything," she says despairingly. "The customer asked for confidentiality, so unless *I'm* Walter Cole, or unless I involve the police. . . ." She looks up slowly. "You know, you hand me a crying five-year-old, and I know exactly what to do. You give me a kid who doesn't know his alphabet, and usually I can have him reading at least a little by the end of the year. People say I'm a comfort to have around at funerals. I'm pretty good beside hospital beds too. But *this* . . . I just don't know. Should I call the cops? Call Bridgie?"

She should be asking Joss, not me, I think. *She's the adult.* But Myrlie's dark eyes are peering at me, searching my face for answers. Because I've got more at stake than Joss does. *It's my parents, my privacy. My secrets.*

I don't know what would happen if we call the police. I don't know what would happen if we didn't. Which action keeps me and my parents safe?

I open my mouth, though I have no idea what I should say. *I'm just good at collecting words,* I think. *Not using them.*

The doorbell rings.

Myrlie scrambles up, seeming relieved by the distraction. I peek down the hallway after her. *Maybe it's my parents,* I think. *Maybe it's the police.*

"Trick or treat!" someone screams out.

It's a pixie, a fairy princess, a werewolf, and a zebra, his black stripes drawn on a white sweatshirt. None of them comes up any higher than Myrlie's waist.

It's Halloween.

"Oh, dear," Myrlie dithers. "I totally forgot it was trick-or-treat night. No . . . wait, don't look so disappointed. I've *got* the candy, I bought it last week, I just don't have it right next to the door. Would you like to step in out of the cold for a minute while I go get it?"

"We're not allowed to go into strangers' houses," the fairy princess says, self-importantly.

A woman emerges out of the dusk behind her.

"It's okay," the woman says. "We know Mrs. Wilker. She was Sammy's teacher, remember?"

The trick-or-treaters step in and I duck my head back into the kitchen, out of sight. I'm not scared of pretend pixies, fairy princesses, werewolves, and zebras, but the woman might be someone else who remembers Elizabeth. Myrlie zips past me and rummages through cupboards, muttering, "I can't believe I forgot about trick or treat. I've been so distracted. . . ." She rips open bags of Snickers, Three Musketeers, Milky Ways, and Skittles, then rushes back out to the kids.

"Here you go," she says. "Oh, don't be shy, take two or three. Bye! Happy Halloween!"

Joss comes into the kitchen through the back door just as Myrlie returns from the front of the house.

"Can you believe it's trick-or-treat night?" Myrlie says. "And I forgot? All the kids were talking about it at school today—they were so excited. But then I saw the newspaper in the teachers' lounge, and everything else went out of my head."

"What'd they say down at the newspaper office?" Joss asks.

"Nancy wasn't allowed to tell me anything," Myrlie says. "Not unless the police got involved, and even then—"

"Don't call the cops," I say quickly, because I've decided all of a sudden. I didn't even want a trick-or-treater's mom to see me. Joss didn't want our names mentioned in the *Sanderfield Reporter*. Why would I want my whole life laid out for some policeman?

"Well, then . . ." Joss says. "Want to go trick-or-treating, Bethany?"

I stare at her in disbelief. One minute I'm being asked to decide Big Questions; the next, I'm supposed to shimmy into some infantile costume and collect candy from strangers?

"No, thanks," I say. And yet, back home, I'd been planning to go trick-or-treating this Halloween. I'd gone last year; my friends and I dressed up like Powerpuff Girls, "Going retro" we called it, just because my friend Molly had been really into the Powerpuff Girls when she was three or four. I'd fought with my parents because my dad insisted on walking with us. "Nobody else's parents are going!" I'd screamed at him. I made him stay several paces behind us, and I'd laughed harder than anyone when Molly joked that he was dressed up to be a stalker "or maybe an undertaker, with that scary face of his."

I was just a kid, last year.

Myrlie is whirling around the kitchen, grabbing bagged salad out of the refrigerator, muttering, "Chicken patties are quick."

"It's going to be a long night," Joss says. "Mom always gets dozens and dozens of trick-or-treaters." She washes her hands and takes a tomato out of Myrlie's hand to begin chopping.

"Can't you just turn out the lights?" I say. "Pretend no one's home?"

Myrlie looks horrified.

"Oh, no. The kids are counting on me," she says.

"But at a time like this? When my parents are . . . ?" I can't finish the sentence. I don't know what my parents are, besides missing, and I can't bring myself to say that.

Myrlie stops zooming around long enough to pat my shoulder.

"Believe me, honey, if I thought I could do anything else to help your parents right now, I'd do it. But just sitting in the dark waiting, pretending to be . . . absent . . . that's not going to help anyone."

The doorbell rings again and Myrlie rushes out to answer it.

"This is her way of dealing with everything," Joss says, sliding the tomato into the salad. "I was so mad at her when I was thirteen, that first year after the accident, when she still wanted to celebrate Christmas and birthdays and Easter and the first robin that showed up in the spring. But . . . it does help. And short of calling the cops, what else are we going to do? You should pass out some of the candy too. It'll cheer you up."

"Only in a mask," I say bitterly.

"No problem," Joss says evenly. "By the end of the evening, Mom will probably be in full costume."

And, strangely, Joss is right. An hour later, after we've gobbled down our chicken patties and salad—interrupted six times by trick-or-treaters—Myrlie is wearing an enchantress's gown and peaked hat, and Joss is dressed like a scarecrow; the trick-or-treaters who come to the door are *ooh*ing and *ahh*ing over them as much as Myrlie and Joss *ooh* and *ahh* over the trick-or-treaters. Then Joss goes back into the kitchen to wash the dishes and Myrlie says, "I've got to go to the bathroom. Can you answer the door the next time it rings?"

"Um . . ." I say. Since dinner, I've spent most of my time slumped down on the couch, out of sight of the door, pretending to watch TV.

"Here," Myrlie says, tossing me one of those fake noses with the dark glasses attached. It's followed by a Raggedy Ann wig that she's dug out of a box. "You need to get into the spirit of the holiday."

I put the glasses over my glasses and arrange the red-yarn hair over my hair, and somehow that does make me feel better. More anonymous, anyway, and anonymous is good right now. When the doorbell rings again three seconds later, I pick up the huge bowl of candy Myrlie left on the table and open the door.

"Trick-or- . . . Wait a minute—you're not Mrs. Wilker," a pumpkin with arms, legs, and a head says.

"No, but I've got the candy," I say. "Want some?"

I drop a Milky Way and a Snickers and a package of Sour Skittles into his bag. He beams at me from beneath green construction-paper tendrils that are evidently supposed to be his pumpkin vine.

"Wow! Thanks!" he says.

After that, Joss and Myrlie and I take turns passing out the candy. Most of the time, Myrlie knows the kids, and makes a game out of trying to guess who's behind some of the masks: "Now, I know that wouldn't be Timmy Rogers in such a scary costume. . . . What's that? It is? Wow, Timmy, that makes me feel a whole lot better, because I know *you'd* be a nice monster."

She chats with the parents, too, and it's like she's truly an enchantress, holding court. It's childish and silly, but I can see why she didn't want to miss Halloween.

By seven thirty, the constant parade of trick-or-treaters has trickled off, and Myrlie, Joss, and I are sitting on the couch with our feet propped up on the coffee table. Myrlie's huge bowl holds only a sprinkling of candy bars.

"I guess it's safe to eat one now, because we're not going to run out," Myrlie says, unwrapping a Snickers. "Want some, Joss? Bethany?"

Joss grabs a Three Musketeers. I start to reach into the bowl, then freeze. What would Elizabeth have chosen? If Elizabeth loved Sour Skittles too, will Joss and Myrlie tell me? Did Sour Skittles even exist twenty years ago?

The doorbell rings again, and Myrlie and Joss groan.

"I'll take care of this one," I say, glad of the distraction. I grab the bowl of candy and head for the door. I open it, thrust out the bowl and start to say, "Here. Take two of whichever kind you . . ."

It's not a trick-or-treater at the door. It's a man, dressed in a business suit.

"Hello, Bethany," he says.

So much for being disguised. I draw the candy bowl back against my chest, holding it like a shield. I squint at the man through my two layers of glasses. He's got close-cropped, graying hair and a heavily lined face. He's a big man—not fat, but bulky. I don't recognize him, exactly, but I know his voice.

He was the man in the car the night before at town square. The one who scared me.

"Tell me," the man says. "Is your dad around?"

I glance frantically back over my shoulder. Joss is already up from the couch, coming to my rescue.

"Who are you looking for?" Joss asks, stationing herself by my side.

"Bethany's father," the man says. "Walter."

I notice he doesn't say a last name.

"Walter's not here," Joss says, raising her chin defiantly.

"Where is he?"

"I can't tell you that," Joss says. "Would you like to leave him a message?"

"Just tell him I stopped by," the man says. "He'll know why."

The man turns around and begins walking away. He's on the steps down from Myrlie's porch when Joss calls out, "Wait a minute—who are you? What's your name?"

The man looks back at us, his eyes narrowed.

"Walter knows who I am," he says, then turns away from us again. He finishes descending the stairs, walks down the sidewalk, opens the gate, begins to slip into the shadows.

"Dalton?" I whisper. I raise my voice, shout out after the man, "Is your name Dalton?"

The man hesitates, just for a moment. He seems startled. But then he keeps walking away from us, into the darkness.

"That's it," Joss says. "I'm calling Bridgie."

—THIRTY·TWO—

It takes the policeman more than an hour to get to Myrlie's house.

"Sorry," he says, easing into a chair at Myrlie's kitchen table. He takes a sip of the coffee she's placed before him. "It being Halloween and all, I had to deal with an egging over on Vine Street. And some kids toilet-papered Mrs. Wade's trees *again*. Now. What seems to be the problem here?"

Myrlie and Joss give him an extremely abridged version of the last five days. They don't say anything about my maybe being a clone or about my father sending $10,000 and fake birth certificates through the mail. The only parts they quote from his letter are the first three sentences: *He is chasing me. He is hunting me down. I thought he would stay in prison.* They don't offer to show Bridgie the letter.

Bridgie listens carefully, the furrow in his brow getting deeper and deeper.

"*Okay*," he says when Joss and Myrlie are done. He looks puzzled. "You want me to put out a warrant for Dr. Krull on child abandonment charges?"

"*No*," Myrlie says. "Walter is just a little . . . troubled right now. It's the man in the car we're worried about."

Bridgie flips back through his notes.

"It's not illegal to offer someone a ride," he says. "It's not illegal to put an ad in the paper, if he's even the one who did it. It's not illegal to knock on someone's door and not leave your name. It's not illegal to look for somebody, and if Dr. Krull feels like he's being chased or hunted, if he's already in some kind of an, uh, unstable mental state already, changing his name and all, well, then that's not this guy's fault."

Bridgie taps his papers with his pen, almost jauntily.

"The man hesitated when I asked if his name was Dalton," I say softly. "I think he's Dalton Van Dyne."

I'm standing behind the policeman, trying to stay out of sight because we've all taken off our costumes now. But when I say this he turns around to peer at me. I bend my head forward so my hair covers my face.

"Uh, right," Bridgie says. "We get a lot of ex-con embezzler-millionaires retiring to Sanderfield."

I decide that if Joss and Bridgie really did date in high school, I hope it was Joss who broke up with him. I hope she broke his heart.

"I know this all sounds a little . . . strange," Myrlie says. "But isn't there anything you can do to help us?"

"Just as a favor, I'll check with the *Reporter* about that ad," Bridgie says. "And I can check with Chicago about the terms of Dalton Van Dyne's release. There might have been some stipulation about him having to stay in the county, or something like that. I can't say I'd mind getting a commendation for finding him here. But . . . it's not very likely that it's him, you know?"

Bridgie gulps down the last of his coffee and stands up. Joss walks him to the front door. Myrlie shakes her head sadly at me.

"Maybe we should have told him everything," she says. "I don't think he took us very seriously. But at least he's helping some."

I shrug and drift out into the hall. I lean against the wall feeling utterly drained. I'm not really trying to eavesdrop, but I can hear Bridgie and Joss talking by the front door.

"Doesn't it freak you out having that girl around?" Bridgie is saying. "Looking so much like Elizabeth?"

I wince, as if he's hit me. I thought I was hiding so well, I thought my hair always covered my face, I thought he hadn't even noticed.

"It's not Bethany's fault," Joss says.

That makes me feel better, but I strain to hear Bridgie's reply.

"I guess," Bridgie says. "You'd think, after all these years, it'd be easier than this. . . . But I still think about her. Every time I go to an accident scene, I think, 'If only those state troopers had gotten to Elizabeth a little faster. . . .' Elizabeth was the first girl I ever kissed, you know that?"

"You didn't really think you were picking out the love of your life when you were seven years old, did you?" Joss says.

I can't hear his response, I'm so horrified.

Wonderful, I think. *Bridgie wasn't Joss's childhood sweetheart. He was Elizabeth's.*

—THIRTY·THREE—

I wake up again in the middle of the night. This time I can't blame the cut on my leg—it's the nightmares that jolt me out of sleep. I'm being chased, and I'm screaming, "Daddy! Mommy! Help me!" But there's no one there. I'm all alone. All I can hear are the footsteps behind me, just like the other night when I was lost—big, heavy footsteps. A man's footsteps.

It wasn't Joss I heard, I tell myself. *It was that man chasing me.*

In the no-man's-land between sleep and full alertness, I'm so certain. I can see exactly how it must have been: The man was chasing me, and when I ran he got into his car and followed me to town square. And then he sat there in the shadows, out of sight, listening to everything Joss and I said. So he could choose the exact right moment to slide up beside us and offer us a ride. . . .

I'm out of bed and rushing for the door because I've got to wake up Myrlie and Joss and tell them what I've figured out.

They've got to call the police again and tell them about this, this is solid evidence we've got now. . . .

And then I'm standing in the hallway, blinking in the harsh light that Myrlie left on for me, just in case, and I'm finally fully awake. I don't have any solid evidence. I just had a nightmare.

I sag against the wall outside my bedroom door and the rest of my nightmare comes back to me.

In another part of my dream a lot of different people were chasing me—Mom and Dad, Joss and Myrlie, gymnastics coaches and Tom Wilker and the grandmother from the videotapes. Even the policeman, Officer Ryan Bridgeman, Bridgie— except he kept changing. One minute he was a little boy, the next he was an adult, the next he was a decrepit old man turning into a skeleton, telling me, "You're the love of my life. . . . We'll be together in death. . . ."

And what I kept screaming at all of them, dead or alive, was, "I am not Elizabeth! *I am not Elizabeth!*"

"I am not Elizabeth," I whisper to the wallpaper.

But I don't really know that; I don't know exactly what it would mean to be a clone. Ever since my mother's bizarre phone call, my mind has shut down in horror every time I've edged close to certain thoughts.

"You will know the truth, and the truth will set you free," I whisper to myself.

I tiptoe over to the stairs and ease down them, clutching the railing the entire way. I remember to skip over the squeaky second step.

Downstairs, in the dark, I turn on the laptop computer and a table lamp. The computer hums itself to life and I stand there in my pool of light, staring at the icons on the screen.

It's just pixels, I tell myself. *Digital bits of information. Sticks and stones can break my bones, but megabytes can never hurt me.*

I sit down at the computer and type two words into a Google search: "Human cloning."

Any computer teacher, any media specialist I've ever dealt with, would be proud of me, because I am so efficient gathering my information. I learn about replacing the nucleus of one cell with the nucleus of another; I learn about rabbits and sheep being used as low-tech artificial wombs for other animals. I do not even feel faint because it is all so scientific and remote. I did not know I could do this so completely, separate my brain and my emotions, so I can think without feeling a thing.

I take a break from cloning research because I am thinking so well now that I have a genius moment. If I want to find out if the man who came to the door tonight really was Dalton Van Dyne, why don't I just look at the embezzler's picture on-line? Okay, it's not exactly a genius moment—the policeman would have thought of it, if he'd taken us seriously. Joss and Myrlie would have thought of it if they hadn't been so upset. But *I'm* the one who's actually typing the words into the search engine. I even get fancy because I don't want to waste any time: I limit my search to pictures taken in the last year.

Nothing comes up.

Well, duh, I think. *He's been in prison. It's not like he's been at summer camp, where they take pictures constantly and splash it all over the Web so your friends back home can see what you've been up to and get jealous.*

Still, I'm a little surprised, because the newspaper and TV stations made such a big deal about his getting out of prison. I'd have thought someone would have aimed a camera at him coming out. I'd have thought he would have had a news conference.

I rewrite my search request, looking for coverage of him leaving prison, but every Web site I can find uses old photos, from before he was sentenced. And staring at those photos... I just can't tell. Dalton Van Dyne was a handsome man thirteen or fourteen years ago, with thick chestnut-colored hair, chiseled features, and a way of looking at the camera as if to say, "Oh, yeah, look at me. I am Somebody Very Important." I am not surprised to see that some of the pictures come from *People* magazine, when he was named one of the world's most eligible bachelors—years ago, before I was born.

The man who stood on Myrlie's porch had the right height and the right build and maybe even the right features, if I am remembering him correctly. But he looked so worn and weary and worried.

Maybe that's what prison did to him, I think. *Or . . . just age.* Images flicker in my mind of the stooped, anxious father I've always known, compared with the young, carefree father in all the videotapes with Elizabeth.

I read more about Dalton Van Dyne because I can't quite bear to go back to my cloning research yet. No matter how good-looking he was, he doesn't sound like a very pleasant person. He was ruthless running Digispur, taking over smaller companies and putting them out of business, laying off scads of employees. He closed down a factory in Tennessee the day before Christmas, and bragged about it. He fired a secretary for spilling coffee on his desk. One of the articles I read calls him "vainglorious," and for the first time since I've arrived at Myrlie's I decide I've discovered a new word I like.

"Vainglorious" is perfect for such a conceited jerk.

I am almost enjoying reading about what a horrible person he was, because I've pretty much decided that he has absolutely nothing to do with me or my parents. My father never would have worked for such a narcissistic, heartless braggart.

And then I find a Dalton Van Dyne quote online that makes my heart stop. An interviewer had asked him about Dolly the cloned sheep:

> "Of course I think it's wonderful," Mr. Van Dyne said. "I wish some of my boys had figured it out. But sheep—that's nothing. Just a dumb farm animal that's going to spend its life standing around eating and pooping. Human cloning's the real deal. The first person who can show off a human clone—with proof—will be hailed as a modern god. He'd replace God. I'd do it in a heartbeat. You know me—I love adulation."

I stare at the words on the screen, and the wall I built between my thoughts and my feelings comes crashing down. I shiver, suddenly fully aware that I'm sitting alone in a dark room in the middle of the night, with just thin doors and fragile windows between me and anyone who might want to harm me. *Joss and Myrlie are right upstairs*, I tell myself, but I can't believe that they would be much protection against a man like Dalton Van Dyne. Because if the man on the porch was Dalton Van Dyne, he doesn't just want to talk to my father. He wants to show me off to the whole wide world, with proof that I am Elizabeth's clone.

He wants to ruin my life.

—THIRTY·FOUR—

"I don't know, Bethany," Joss says, squinting at the picture on the small screen. "I guess that could be the guy we saw."

"But not for sure," Myrlie says.

I woke them up, Joss and Myrlie, and now they're huddled around the computer with me, looking at the old pictures of Dalton Van Dyne. Myrlie's hair is sticking up in odd places and Joss has dark circles under her eyes that somehow make her look like a little girl again. Myrlie hugs her robe more tightly around her waist.

"Where's that quote that scared you so much?" she asks, rubbing the sleep from her eyes.

I call up Van Dyne's words again, and Joss and Myrlie read silently.

"But, see, down here, Bethany, he says, 'Don't you think the world needs about fifty more of me?'" Joss says, pointing lower on the screen, to a paragraph I hadn't read. "He's talking about wanting to clone himself."

"It's just talk," Myrlie says gently. She rests a hand on my shoulder. "He was a public figure and he ran his mouth off about all sorts of things. It's got nothing to do with you."

Except that word "clone," I think.

I see Myrlie and Joss exchanging glances that seem to say, *The poor kid's been under a lot of strain lately. Surely we can excuse a little paranoia.*

I don't want their sympathy. I want action.

"Let's see what Bridgie has to say before we get too bent out of shape," Joss suggests.

"Fine," I say bitterly. I reach out and stab at the button that clears the screen of greedy, selfish Dalton Van Dyne and his desire to replace God.

So my only protection is a kindergarten teacher and a ninety-eight-pound female minister, I think. *And they don't even believe I'm in any danger.*

Joss yawns.

"What time is it, anyway?" she asks.

"Nearly six," Myrlie says, squinting at the clock. "I might as well stay up, now. Do the two of you want breakfast or are you going back to bed?"

I stare at her, openmouthed. How can she think about food at a time like this? I remember what she said the night before: *You hand me a crying five year old, and I know exactly what to do. You give me a kid who doesn't know his alphabet, and usually I can have him reading at least a little by the end of the year. People say I'm a comfort to have around at funerals. I'm pretty good beside hospital beds too. But this. I just don't know.* My parents left me with the wrong person. If they loved me as much as they always said they did, they would have had a better backup plan.

"I—" Joss starts to answer, but just then the doorbell peals out.

All three of us freeze—Joss midsentence, Myrlie halfway to the kitchen, me in the midst of reaching for the computer to shut it down. For all their cavalier talk a few minutes ago, they look just as stricken as I feel. Then Myrlie turns and moves briskly toward the door.

Maybe she is brave, after all, I think.

Myrlie peeks out the window, then yanks the door open.

"Bridgie?" she says incredulously.

She opens the screen door for him too, and he steps in, onto her hardwood floor. He's got a piece of paper in his hand, but he's holding it facedown. Even last night, after he'd investigated egged houses and toilet-papered trees, his uniform looked crisp and professional. Now he's bleary-eyed and his uniform is rumpled, as if he'd just thrown it on. His shirt cuffs aren't even buttoned.

"I hope this isn't too early," he says. "I wouldn't have stopped in except I saw your lights on."

"No, no, that's fine," Myrlie says. "As you can see, we're up. We're just not all . . ."—she glances down at her robe—"dressed."

"Have a seat," Joss says.

Bridgie perches on the edge of the couch. Myrlie and Joss settle around him. I stay by the computer.

"I was going to look into your questions first thing this morning," Bridgie says. "But I couldn't sleep." He glances over at me, and looks away fast. "I got up in the middle of the night and checked my e-mail. And there was this bulletin . . ."

"A bulletin?" Myrlie repeats, leaning forward.

Bridgie nods. "It's one of those cross-jurisdictional courtesy things. Police departments notify other police departments when suspected criminals or ex-cons move into their area." He fiddles with the edge of the paper he's holding. "Dalton Van Dyne wasn't ordered to stay in the Chicago area as a condition of his release. He just has to let the authorities know where he goes."

"He *is* in Sanderfield," I breathe.

Bridgie peers over at me, but he still can't quite make his eyes meet mine. He shrugs apologetically.

"Yes," he says. He flips over the paper in his hand. "Is this the man you saw?"

—THIRTY·FIVE—

I rush over to the couch and crane my neck to see the picture of Dalton Van Dyne as he looks now, after prison. It's a grainy, security-camera-type shot, printed out from a computer, but it's clear that Dalton Van Dyne doesn't have chestnut-colored hair anymore, he doesn't ooze confidence, he won't make *People* magazine's list of most eligible bachelors this year. In this picture, Dalton Van Dyne has ugly gray, grizzled, close-cropped hair, and his worn, heavily lined face stares warily at the camera.

I have no doubts now.

"That's him," Joss says grimly.

Bridgie nods, as if he's had his worst fears confirmed.

"Why would he come *here?*" he asks. "Why would he be looking for Dr. Krull?"

Joss and Myrlie look at me, and I can tell they're wondering if I'll advance the same theory I woke them up for, just an hour ago. Would they tell Bridgie the theory themselves, even if they don't believe it?

I bite my lip, all my fears fighting in my head.

"My father might have worked for Dalton Van Dyne," I say hesitantly. "Joss and I found a link on the Web yesterday."

"Let me see," Bridgie says.

Bridgie follows me back to the computer and seconds later I have my father's name up on the screen, in the list of supposedly fictitious employees in a supposedly nonexistent office: ". . . Sandra Despre, Walter Krull, Antonio Perez, and Michael Sciullo never existed . . ."

Bridgie backs away from the computer shaking his head.

"This doesn't make sense," Bridgie said. "If Dr. Krull really worked for Van Dyne, and got a salary from him, then Van Dyne didn't steal all that money. His defense attorney would have called Dr. Krull and the others to the witness stand to prove that Van Dyne wasn't an embezzler. Or at least to prove that he didn't embezzle *everything*. He wouldn't have gotten such a long prison sentence if he hadn't taken so much money."

"Maybe that's why Uncle Walter changed his name and disappeared," Joss says. "To avoid testifying."

"But why?" Myrlie asks, sounding even more bewildered than ever. "Why would Walter do that?"

I remember Joss telling me that "Why?" was the question that religion answered; I remember telling her I didn't know what my parents believed. But my father always told me to treat people fairly—when I was a little kid refusing to share my toys, he always told me I had to think about other people's feelings. Were those just meaningless words? Was he secretly the type of person who would let someone go to prison for a long time when he could have spoken up and stopped it?

I'm back to the same question Myrlie had asked: *Why would Walter do that?*

Bridgie's watching my aunt and cousin. He clicks on the mouse to erase the whole Van Dyne story, and the screenful of disturbing words is replaced by Myrlie's soothing wallpaper: a field of flowers.

"This is upsetting you ladies," Bridgie says quietly. "I want you to know that the Sanderfield Police will be keeping an eye on Mr. Van Dyne. And we'll have extra patrols on your block, just in case."

"Thank you," Myrlie says.

I'm not comforted. I want an around-the-clock guard by Myrlie's door. I want Dalton Van Dyne arrested.

Some small voice in the back of my head whispers, *But what if he's really done nothing wrong? What if my father's the true criminal?*

—THIRTY·SIX—

There's nothing to do after Bridgie leaves. Myrlie and Joss loll on the couch and I sprawl in the computer chair, and the way we're all sitting reminds me of crime scenes in movies, the chalk drawings on pavement showing where the bodies fell.

Shell-shocked, I think. *We're shell-shocked.*

Having Bridgie show up with his official notification and his picture of Dalton Van Dyne—newly released from prison, mysteriously appearing in Sanderfield, asking for my dad—is the first concrete proof we've had that my parents aren't crazy. (Not completely crazy, anyway.) I miss that explanation now; I long for the time when I thought my parents were merely insane.

"You didn't tell him," I murmur to Myrlie and Joss. "You didn't tell Bridgie that my mom says they cloned Elizabeth, that that might be the link between my dad and Van Dyne, that I might be—"

"Bridgie's not conducting an investigation," Myrlie says. "He wasn't seeking information. He just wants to protect us."

Joss turns her head and looks at her mother, and I can't read the expression on either of their faces. I remember a movie I saw once, where a murderer confessed his crime to a priest, but the priest wasn't allowed to tell anyone. It was something about the murderer's sins being between him and God, and the priest had taken an oath of confidentiality. Was being a minister like being a priest? Do teachers ever promise to keep secrets too?

"I know how it must have been," I say dully, because I think I've just now figured out the final pieces in the puzzle. "Dalton Van Dyne paid my dad to . . . to produce me. Van Dyne just wanted to brag to the world, 'Look what I made happen! Look what my money did!' But then Van Dyne got caught stealing other money, and he didn't want anyone else to get the credit for the first cloned human, so he didn't say anything about what my dad had done. And then when Van Dyne went to prison, my parents took me away, and they kept changing their names so he couldn't track them down. But Van Dyne found out where they were, and they thought they could hide me here and they could be like decoys or something, running away, throwing him off from finding me. But Van Dyne didn't fall for it. He found me first. Because I kept calling my dad's cell phone from here that first day, probably. But now he's just biding his time, waiting to get his proof, maybe, before he steals me back. . . ."

I wait for Myrlie and Joss to protest, to say, "That's ridiculous, you're imagining things, that can't be the explanation." But they just stare at me uncertainly. Something else strikes me.

"Oh, no," I moan. "Where's Elizabeth buried?"

"In Sanderfield Cemetery," Joss says. "On the west side of town. We would have passed it Monday when we went to the state park, except that I took a detour."

She's looking at me as if she has no idea why I asked.

"Don't you see?" I say. "He could go there, he could . . ." I can't quite bring myself to say the horrific words: *dig up her body*. This is too grisly, even worse than the graverobbers in *Tom Sawyer*, even worse than ghost stories my friends and I whispered at sleepovers. "He could get his proof at the cemetery," I choke out. I struggle up from my chair, my leg throbbing, my muscles aching from raking nearly the entire yard yesterday, except for the area around Elizabeth's tree. "We have to go there, we have to stop him. . . ."

I'm trying to race for the door, but I feel like I'm back in one of my nightmares, where I run and run but just can't get away from everyone who's chasing me. Myrlie reaches out and grabs my arm.

"No," she says. Her voice and her grip are both so solid and firm, the fight goes out of me and I sag against her. "None of us are going to the cemetery," she says. "I'll call Bridgie and let him know—"

"Don't tell him everything," I beg. "Please. I don't want him to know anything about me being Elizabeth's clone."

I'm so ashamed, suddenly. Joss said none of this was my fault, but I just can't believe it. The way Bridgie looks at me, it's like he blames me for everything. It's like Elizabeth was a star, and I'm just a piece of dust trying to impersonate her, trying to steal the love people had for her, trying to bring back all their grief and rub their faces in it.

"I won't tell him that," Myrlie says. "I promise. You can listen."

I trail her to the kitchen and all but press my head against the phone receiver while she talks.

"Bridgie?" Myrlie says. "Bethany thinks Van Dyne might go to Sanderfield Cemetery."

I hear a crackle on the other end that's probably Bridgie saying, "Why would he do that?"

"It's just a guess," Myrlie says. "But think about it. If this guy's mad at Walter and Hillary, wouldn't vandalizing Elizabeth's grave be a particularly cruel form of revenge?"

I pull back from the phone, I'm so amazed at Myrlie. She isn't lying, but she also isn't giving anything away. As far as I'm concerned, she's a genius.

"Uh-huh," she's saying to Bridgie. "Well, that's not a surprise."

I peer at Myrlie's troubled face. Then I understand.

"They found out that Van Dyne really was the one who placed the ad in the newspaper," I say aloud.

Myrlie winces and nods at me, though she's still listening to Bridgie on the phone.

Van Dyne probably knows all my father's aliases, I think. *He knows all about us.*

"We have had a few phone calls where the person on the other end just hangs up," Myrlie says.

Was that Van Dyne too? I wonder. I remember Sunday morning, picking up the phone and crying out, "Daddy, why didn't you call yesterday?" before I even said hello. Was Van Dyne on the other end of the line?

I've lost track of Myrlie's phone conversation. Then I realize her voice has changed now. She almost sounds happy.

"Oh, really?" she's saying into the phone. "That's great. Thanks."

When she hangs up, I stare at her, waiting for her to explain what's so great. Maybe they've found my parents; maybe they've arrested Dalton Van Dyne for phone harassment and sent him back to prison for the rest of his life; maybe they've just happened to have turned up blood tests that prove that Elizabeth and I are two totally different people. . . .

But Myrlie's expression is conflicted.

"Bridgie says he called the state association of small-town police divisions, just for some advice. One thing led to another, and it turns out prosecutors always felt they were missing something in the case against Van Dyne, thirteen years ago, and, well . . ."

"What?" I demand.

"The FBI's going to be here too, watching Van Dyne. Protecting us."

Nosing around, I think. *Talking to people. Finding out more than I want anyone else to know.*

—THIRTY·SEVEN—

Joss and Myrlie make no attempt to keep me from sitting around fidgeting and worrying today. They're sitting around fidgeting and worrying too, although sometimes their eyes close. I'm not sure if they're sleeping or praying.

I can't do either. I sit by the front window and peer out. Myrlie calls her school to say she's taking another day off work, and I watch the school buses come and go. Every hour or so a police car creeps by. People walk their dogs; they push babies in strollers. Two women stop on the corner to chat, while their toddlers play in a pile of leaves. They cast worried glances at the dark clouds in the sky, and move on.

That could have been Myrlie and Mom, thirty years ago, I think. I bet anything the two of them stood in that very spot chatting, while Joss and Elizabeth played in the leaves. Sanderfield was Elizabeth's world, just an ordinary place to grow up, a place where grandparents planted trees to celebrate new babies in the family. But Sanderfield wasn't enough for Elizabeth; she wanted to dazzle the entire nation, the entire planet.

Sanderfield would be enough for me, I think. *Just to be an ordinary kid in an ordinary place . . .*

Lightning flashes and thunder cracks and the skies open, sending down sheets of rain. The rain brings down a torrent of leaves from all the trees in Myrlie's front yard. Everything is falling down, falling apart. And through the glaze of rain and falling leaves, I see a dark car glide by.

"There he is!" I shriek. "He's right outside."

Joss comes and stands beside me, and together we watch the car slip out of sight.

"Call the police!" I say.

Joss shakes her head.

"They can't arrest him just for driving down a street," she says.

The phone rings, and I think maybe Joss is wrong; maybe this is Bridgie telling us they've captured Van Dyne and we're safe and secure once again. I sprint into the kitchen and grab the phone before Joss or Myrlie even have a chance to move.

"Bethany?"

It's my mother's voice and, miracle of miracles, she knows who I am.

"Oh, Mom," I whimper.

"He doesn't know I'm calling, I'm not supposed to call, but I had to say good-bye."

"No, Mom, you—"

Myrlie's standing beside me and she's got her hand outstretched, like I'm supposed to give her the phone. I press it tighter against my ear and turn my back on her.

"I know, honey," Mom says sorrowfully. "I don't want to say good-bye either, but I understand now. Tomorrow is your birthday. We'll lose you at thirteen too, just like Elizabeth. It's just meant to be."

I've forgotten about my birthday; I've lost all track of days and dates since coming to Myrlie's house. I can't imagine birthdays anymore, or having such a simple life that I could blow out candles on a cake and believe that my wishes would come true.

The way Mom says "birthday" gives me chills. It sounds like she's expecting me to die.

"No," I say. "You don't have to say good-bye. Come back—"

"Don't be sad," Mom says. "I'm not sad now. We had you for almost thirteen years, and that was . . . more than we deserved. It was cheating. But I've loved every moment of your life, every second we had with you. You're so special to us—"

"Mom, listen," I say. "It doesn't have to be this way. None of this is meant to be. There's still time for you and Daddy to save me. Let me talk to Daddy. I have to tell him—Dalton Van Dyne is *here,* here in Sanderfield, asking for Daddy. Please, Mom, if you really love me, you'll let me talk to Daddy."

"I can't . . . ," Mom begins.

Out of the corner of my eye, I see a huge streak of lightning; seconds later I hear such a loud boom of thunder that it seems like the whole world is being split in two. The lights in the kitchen flicker and dim and then zap out entirely, plunging the room into a dusky darkness.

"Mom?" I shout into the phone. "Mom? Mom, *please,* answer me. *Please."*

Nothing but silence comes back to me. Silence and emptiness. The phone is dead.

THIRTY-EIGHT

I whirl on Myrlie.

"It's all your fault!" I scream. "Having a stupid landline! A cell phone would still be working, I'd still be talking to my mom!" I'm pounding the receiver on the counter, so hard Myrlie probably can't even hear my words over the banging. "She was going to let me talk to my dad—she was! They . . . love . . . me!"

The hand that's slamming the phone against the counter is throbbing now; I look down and see that I've missed the counter and scraped my knuckles. I'm bleeding.

I'm losing Elizabeth's blood, I think stupidly—stupidly, because isn't it my blood now?

"Now, Bethany . . ." Myrlie says soothingly, and that makes me madder because I don't want to be soothed. I can barely see Myrlie in the dim light coming in from the windows, and that reminds me that the electricity is still out.

"Oh, no!" I say. "What if Van Dyne cut the power lines and the phone lines, and now he's going to attack us, when we can't call for help. That's how it always happens in movies. . . ."

"It was lightning," Joss says calmly behind me. "Van Dyne can't control the lightning."

She lays a hand on my shoulder and I shake it off.

"She was calling to say good-bye," I wail. "They're giving up on me, letting me go—they'd let me die! They don't care what happens to me anymore, they're just gone. . . ."

"There, there," Myrlie says, and she pats my shoulder, then slides her hands down to my arms. I feel like a wild beast being captured. I jerk away.

"They can't protect me now, nobody can protect me, he's going to get me, it's not safe. . . ."

I'm sobbing now, just like my mother. Except my sobs are loud—I'm surprised Dalton Van Dyne and the police and the FBI agents and all of Sanderfield can't hear me. I'm screaming and wailing and I don't even realize I've begun to chant, "I am not Elizabeth! I am not Elizabeth!" until I hear the words echoing back to me.

Joss and Myrlie aren't trying to calm me down anymore. They're just standing there waiting—waiting for the lights to come back on or for Van Dyne to attack or for me to pull myself together.

"I can't," I whimper, not screaming or wailing or sobbing anymore only because I don't have the energy for it. *Pull myself together* makes me think of a computer-animated skit I saw once of cartoon hands picking up cartoon arms and legs and feet and a head, and putting all the pieces together. The title of the skit was "A Self-made Man." But I'm not self-made. I'm more like Humpty Dumpty: Now that I've fallen apart I don't think anyone could put me back together again.

Joss and Myrlie are still watching me.

"I'm sorry," I whisper.

"I know," Myrlie says. "We are too."

—THIRTY·NINE—

I fall asleep. This is my way of letting go, of giving up. If I'm Elizabeth's clone, so be it; if my parents are never coming back, so be it; if Van Dyne is about to reveal my identity, what can I do to stop him? I lie on the couch in the living room and drift in and out of consciousness. Myrlie and Joss tiptoe by, carrying candles, because the lights still aren't back on.

I don't know how many hours later it is when Joss leans over me. "Okay, that's enough," she says. "Time's up."

"What?" I say. I struggle to sit up, but my head is too woozy. I fall back against the cushion.

"Believe me, I know all about wallowing in misery," Joss says. "I was something of an expert in it myself, twenty years ago. But you've got to set some limits. Get up."

She slides her hands under my shoulders, pries me up into a sitting position. My head spins, then clears.

"Here's what we're going to do," Joss says. "First, you're

going to get dressed. Mom has already used my cell phone to order pizza from a place that still has electricity. So we're going to have a great dinner. And then we're going out."

"Out?" I repeat. I glance down at my clothes. I'm still wearing pajamas. I've had them on all day.

"Out," Joss says firmly. "Sanderfield has a Harvest Festival every year, the day after Halloween. I just checked online—using the last of the laptop's batteries, I might add—and the festival is still on. They have electricity downtown, the rain's stopped, we're going."

I reach up and cover my face with my hands.

"People will see me," I say. "They'll ask questions, like that woman at the Y did."

"Lots of kids wear costumes and masks to this. We can find something to disguise you, if you want."

I think about how Dalton Van Dyne still knew who I was the night before, when I was wearing the Raggedy Ann hair and the fake nose.

"What if Van Dyne finds out where we're going?" I ask.

Joss shakes her head sadly.

"Van Dyne knows where you are right now. If he wanted to do something . . ."

Joss doesn't have to finish that sentence.

"What if my mom calls again while we're gone and we miss it?" I ask.

"The phone lines are still down," Joss says. "She can't call."

I'm out of arguments. It's not that I want to go anywhere, but I don't have the will to resist. I put on clothes—blue jeans, a striped rugby shirt—all from my old life, my old self. They hang on me as if I'm a scarecrow.

The pizza arrives and it's so thick and greasy I can barely swallow. But in the candlelight, Joss and Myrlie pretend not to notice. They try to joke around and be merry, telling stories about how the owner of Sanderfield Pizza went to Italy once and pronounced all the food there "horrible and unfit for human consumption."

"And that explains a lot about the pizza we're eating right now," Joss laughs.

"It's not *bad*," Myrlie protests. "It's just not very authentic."

I don't laugh along. I don't even talk. But when the dishes are cleared away and Myrlie's grabbing her purse and her car keys, I say one word: "Mask."

"Oh, that's right," Joss says. "Bethany wanted to go in costume."

"No problem," Myrlie says.

She goes down to the basement and pulls out the same box of costumes we used last night. Myrlie has practically every theme covered: witches and fairy princesses and flower faces and hippies and the Cat in the Hat.

"What can I say? Thirty years of teaching kindergarten, you accumulate quite a collection," Myrlie tells me. "You should see all my 'Apple for the Teacher' stationery."

I sort through the box twice, and end up making my first independent decision of the evening. When we settle into Myrlie's car fifteen minutes later, I'm wearing my swim cap and swim goggles.

"Can you see well enough out of those things?" Myrlie asks. "Without your glasses, I mean."

"They're prescription goggles," I say, and it's like I'm claiming some piece of my old identity. *I'm a serious enough swimmer that*

I own prescription swim goggles. I'm a swimmer, and Elizabeth would never dip a toe in the water.

It's a short drive to the Harvest Festival, because it's held in the town square.

"We should have just walked," Myrlie complains when we have to park a block and a half away, after circling the blocked-off streets twice.

Joss gives her a look, and this is the first sign I've seen all night that they're afraid too, beneath their masks of jokes and fake merriment. If we'd walked, we would have been alone and defenseless for four or five blocks, on dark streets with dead streetlights, under stark, leafless trees.

We get out of the car and join the crowds streaming toward the square. People seem to be in high spirits, laughing off the violent storm and the power outage.

"Oh, Myrlie, I'm so sorry you used up a whole personal day," a woman in the crowd says to Myrlie. "We were only at school about an hour and then they sent us all home."

"Oh, well," Myrlie says gamely.

We turn the corner into town square, and it's been transformed. A small Ferris wheel, a merry-go-round, and a Tilt-A-Whirl are scattered around the blocked-off streets, between booths selling lemonade, cotton candy, Elephant Ears, and deep-fried Snickers. Because I am seeing everything through my swim goggles, I feel like I am underwater. Kids in monster masks float up beside me then stream away into the crowd. The lights of the Ferris wheel spin before my eyes; shrieks rise up from the Tilt-A-Whirl. One child stops screaming only long enough to beg, "Mommy, can I ride it again?"

It is strange to be out of the house. It is strange to be walking around, but hidden beneath my cap and goggles. It is strange to see a crowd gathered around a "Show Your Strength—Amaze Your Friends" game on the very spot where I fell two nights ago, just inches from the memorial to Tom Wilker.

If it's strange for me, how strange is it for Myrlie, to see people laughing and playing practically on top of the tribute to her husband's death?

I watch a teenage boy, all swagger and attitude, as he grips the hammer and swings it over his shoulder, bringing it down squarely on the target. A ball shoots to the top, ringing the bell. Lights flash up and down the pole, and a barker cries out, "Ladies and gentlemen! We have a winner!"

I want to play my "If I were a movie set designer" game, because this scene would be perfect for some heartwarming Disney family drama, some story of a small-town carnival where the worst danger anyone faces is from eating too much cotton candy and maybe getting a stomachache. But I know too much about this scene. I know it's built on top of a tombstone and sorrow and pain; I know Myrlie and Joss are scared, walking beside me; I know I would not be brave enough to be here if I couldn't hide behind my goggles. I find I can blink and see the world around me in many different ways. Blink once and I see an innocent, lighthearted carnival, the lights of the Ferris wheel arcing high overhead, the merry-go-round music tooting happily. Blink again and all the monster masks leer at me, the darkened buildings beyond the carnival hunch ominously at the edge of my vision, the newly bared tree limbs reach desperately for the sky.

I blink again, and I see my parents.

—FORTY—

They are stumbling toward me: two sad, old people clutching one another. If my father looked wrong on Myrlie's cheerful porch a week ago, the two of them are totally out of place at this festival. They're like apparitions. For a minute, I think I am imagining them, my vision distorted by the goggles. But the crowd divides around them, giving wide berth to such a pathetic, broken, defeated-looking pair. If I am imagining them, so is everyone else.

Then my parents see me and their faces light up with joy and relief, with an echo of grief, just like always. At least I understand the mix of joy and grief, now. It's because when they see me, they also see Elizabeth.

My mother mouths something—maybe "I told him," maybe "I love you." Really, I've known all along that they love me. It's just that their love has always been rooted in sorrow and fear.

"You came," I say. "You came to protect me."

I'm not sure they can hear me over the noise of the crowd, the shouts of glee and mock terror coming from the Tilt-A-Whirl. They aren't looking at me anymore. They're looking beyond me, behind me. I turn around. A tall, bulky man with gray, grizzled hair raises one eyebrow in my direction.

Dalton Van Dyne has been following me.

But he's looking past me too; he's staring at my parents. I realize too late that I was the true decoy. I might not have been in any danger at all from Van Dyne—he'd scared me just to get to my parents. He must have known I would have panicked; he must have known that I would have pleaded, "Come back! Save me!"

I freeze, watching Van Dyne. I have a sick feeling in the pit of my stomach. I'm half-expecting him to pull a gun out of his pocket, to kill us all. But he only stops and yells at my parents, "Where is he?"

My father stiffens, then shakes my mother's hand from his arm and tries to pull himself up to his full height. The way he's standing reminds me of the buildings in Western movies, with two-story facades in the front and crumbling one-story shacks in the back.

"I don't owe you anything," my father says. "I sent back your money."

"I don't care about the money," Van Dyne says. "Where is he?"

My father doesn't answer.

Behind Van Dyne, a few men step forward, and I realize they must be the FBI agents. *Plainclothesmen*, I think, the word coming from some old book I must have read a long time ago. *Agents going incognito.* But they're the only ones who step forward; everyone else in the crowd seems to shift away, as if they sense danger. I know from books and movies and TV that the FBI agents probably have tiny tape recorders hidden in their pockets, copying down every word, every sound.

"All I thought about the past thirteen years was my boy," Van Dyne says, his voice choked with pain. "Did he know where I was? Would he be ashamed?"

The carnival noise seems to recede behind me. I'm straining to hear Van Dyne's every word. It's like we're in a fishbowl now. People are staring.

"On bad days, I worried that he was having the same kind of childhood I'd had, all beatings, no hugs," Van Dyne says, stepping closer to me, to my parents. "On good days, I imagined that he was with better parents than I could ever be. But I checked around, and I could never find a trace of him. You hid him so well. I only want my son. I'll never bother you again if you give him back. Please, I beg of you, tell me where he is." For a second it seems like he's about to reach out and grab my father by the shoulders, maybe to shake him, maybe to punch him. But then Van Dyne drops his arms, drops his head and mutters, "I have to find him, to warn him. I have to find my . . . younger self."

Perhaps I am the only one close enough to hear his final words. We've formed an odd geometry in the midst of the crowd: Joss and Myrlie are flanking my parents now, the FBI agents are hovering behind Van Dyne, and I am caught in the middle. But the balance shifts when I hear those words. I suddenly understand what Van Dyne wants from my parents. I suddenly understand how my old theories were wrong.

"You paid him to clone you," I whisper to Van Dyne. "You're looking for your clone."

I remember Joss pointing out Van Dyne's quote on the computer screen: *Don't you think the world needs about fifty more of me?* I remember how conceited and self-centered he'd been, thirteen years ago.

I look back at my parents, and they seem to be shrinking before my eyes. *That's what my dad lied about,* I think. *This is the moment he's been afraid of for my entire life. That's why they're cowering in fear. They think they deserve whatever Van Dyne is going to do to them.*

I step closer to Van Dyne. All this time I've been wondering who I really am, what my actual last name is, whether I'm just a lesser copy of Elizabeth. But none of that matters now. My identity doesn't depend on names or genes. It depends on what I do—what I do right now, to protect my parents.

I whip the swim cap and goggles from my head. My hair unfurls behind me, flowing freely in the breeze. Around me I hear gasps and whispers, "She looks just like Elizabeth, the girl who died. . . . How can it be?"

I stare straight into Van Dyne's eyes.

"Your clone doesn't exist," I tell him. "They made me instead. I am the clone."

I am not used to looking at the world without goggles or glasses or anything else hiding me, changing the way I look, changing the way I see. So much around me is a blur—the FBI agents, the crowd, the games, the lights of the Ferris wheel. But I'm close enough to see Van Dyne clearly—Dalton Van Dyne the powerful, the terrifying, my own personal bogeyman.

And Dalton Van Dyne is crying.

—EPILOGUE—

I am thirteen now. My birthday was the strangest
one of my life—no cake, no candles, no presents. It turns out
there were reporters as well as FBI agents following Van Dyne,
and they heard every word I said. So on my birthday we were
under siege at Myrlie's house: the phone ringing constantly,
the reporters and photographers pounding at the door. Finally,
my father went out late in the afternoon to tell them all, "I have
no comment to make. Please leave my family alone."

"But, Dr. Krull—it is Krull, isn't it? Don't you want to prove
this incredible claim your daughter made?" a reporter yelled at
him. "Don't you want to take your place with the great scientists of history?"

My father looked out at the crowd of journalists jostling to
cover one of the biggest stories of their lifetime. In the TV
footage, which I have seen now many times, he stands straight
and proud, almost defiant. His eyes are hooded but guileless.

"I already have everything I want," he said, and turned around and shut the door of Myrlie's house behind him. No TV camera captured what he did next: gathered Mom and me into a hug.

It may sound strange, but Dalton Van Dyne was there at Myrlie's house the day of my thirteenth birthday too. Joss had long talks with him at the kitchen table, and she came out and reported, "That's the loneliest man I've ever met in my entire life. He thought a clone would be the only person who could possibly love him."

Joss still talks to Van Dyne a lot; last month she flew to Chicago to help him open a group home for troubled teenaged boys. The media had a field day with Van Dyne's transformation: EX-CON EMBEZZLER TURNS LIFE AROUND, the headlines went. And, FORMER BILLIONAIRE DOWN TO ONE PAIR OF SHOES; GIVES ALL ELSE TO CHARITY. But he, too, refuses to comment on any cloning stories.

That hasn't kept the media away, of course. A *Chicago Tribune* reporter tracked down the other "fictitious" Digispur employees who worked with my dad, and some of them talked. One of those TV news magazines has filed a lawsuit trying to get access to tissue samples from Elizabeth and me, to prove or disprove my cloning "once and for all." Six months ago, that would have seemed like one of my worst nightmares. But now, it's amazing how distant that all seems, how easily I can get past it.

I revealed myself, after all.

And I know the whole truth now. I know there are no more surprises lurking out there. My parents told me everything I hadn't already figured out.

Because I've seen the videotape of my parents from more than twenty years ago, because I know about Elizabeth, I can picture my father approaching Dalton Van Dyne in the late 1990s. "You want a clone?" my father asked him. "I can do that."

It was a lie born of desperate hope and bravado. Elizabeth's only remaining living cells had been frozen for years at that point. My father had worked in labs around the world, learning techniques and possibilities, but he'd never been the boss, he'd never had a chance to try to clone Elizabeth.

Dalton Van Dyne put him in charge of his own lab.

At first, my father had every intention of creating two clones, one of Dalton Van Dyne, one of Elizabeth. But then Van Dyne was arrested for "accounting irregularities" at Digispur, and it was clear that the secret lab was about to be closed down. Errol Schwartz, the man poised to replace Van Dyne as Digispur CEO, was virulently opposed to all biological research. Van Dyne wired my father huge sums of money with the message, "For raising my boy. Don't tell anyone!" And my father stood in a deserted lab and made a choice. Van Dyne, he thought, would probably get another chance. Elizabeth's frozen cells wouldn't. Four cloned embryos went to four different surrogate mothers, and all the embryos contained nuclei from Elizabeth's cells.

The surrogate mothers went to four different places around the country, because Van Dyne's trial was going on then, and my father was already growing paranoid. When it came time for the babies to be born, they all arrived at the same time. And then, one by one, during their first twenty-four hours of life, they all began to die.

Except one.

Me.

"It's because you were my baby," my mom interrupted when my dad was telling me this story.

"What do you mean?" I asked, confused. My mother by then wasn't crying anymore, but she was loopy with medication, prone to forgetting who any of us were.

"I gave birth to you," my mother said. "I was one of the surrogate mothers. Your father said I was too old—but I wasn't. I was the only one whose baby lived."

And then I understood that my actual birth had gone pretty much the way I'd always thought, long before I'd heard about cloning. And that made me feel better, to be that normal, at least.

My father told everyone he'd worked with that all the cloned babies died, and then he changed his name and tried to erase his tracks. He kept all the birth certificates, and as a family we went through a lot of names those first few years.

"But once you were old enough to know your last name, we didn't want to confuse you," he assured me earnestly.

In the beginning, they had wanted an exact copy of Elizabeth. But they were so happy to have me that they kept trying to make my life easier than Elizabeth's had been, more enjoyable. And they were so scared of losing me—so easily reminded that they'd lost Elizabeth—that they did everything they could to protect me.

My father kept Van Dyne's money because he didn't know how to send it back until Van Dyne got out of prison. But sending it back didn't make him feel any better. It only made him more paranoid, more worried that Van Dyne could track him down.

That's why he took me to Myrlie.

"We always thought of Sanderfield as safe," my father explained. "A haven we didn't deserve anymore. But you were innocent. You could go back when we couldn't. We never dreamed that Van Dyne would follow you instead of us."

This was before my father went into therapy, and the therapist could point out all the inconsistencies in my father's logic, the dangers that lurked for me in Sanderfield. If my parents had been thinking rationally, Sanderfield is the last place they would have left me—Sanderfield, where anyone might recognize me, where practically every adult knew more about my family than I did. But my parents desperately wanted to avoid putting me through all their panic and fear, sleeping in a different hotel every night, driving endless loops across Kansas and Nebraska, Iowa and Missouri and Illinois—coming back to mail a letter, running away at every imagined hint of danger. Myrlie, in the end, was the only person they trusted to protect me.

"And maybe subconsciously they were acknowledging that it was time for you to know the truth," my therapist said. "Maybe they had motives in taking you to Sanderfield that even they couldn't understand."

Maybe.

As you can tell, I have a therapist now too. So does my mom. We're just your ordinary, typical American family, who could keep the entire psychiatric industry in business all by ourselves.

My father did show the psychiatrists the proof of my cloning.

"Just so you know we're not delusional," he said.

But that's as far as the proof has gone. My parents' attorneys are confident that we can hold off the onslaught of the news media. And they're confident that my father will never be charged for his connection to the Digispur embezzling scandals. The FBI has been investigating him; but, strangely, all they seem to care about is the money.

"It doesn't make sense," I complained to the therapist last week. "The lawyers say my dad's biggest mistake was sending the money back to Dalton Van Dyne, because that could look like money laundering, or something. Still, they think they can get him off because he didn't have any—what do they call it?—criminal intent. But sending the money back was my dad's way of trying to make things right. And Van Dyne gave it all back to Digispur. Why isn't anyone concerned about my dad lying to Van Dyne? And what about the cloning?"

"Cloning wasn't illegal fourteen years ago," the therapist said mildly. "And in this context, lying isn't a federal crime." She raised one of her overly plucked eyebrows. "Bethany . . . are you angry with your parents?"

Of course I am. Of course I'm not. Why can't she understand?

I much prefer the talks Joss and I have. I kind of see now what she means when she says that life always wins in the end. Elizabeth died, and because of that Joss became a minister and Ryan Bridgeman became a police officer trying to help other people. My parents cheated Van Dyne, but now Van Dyne is helping troubled kids.

"Was my dad right or wrong to clone Elizabeth?" I asked Joss once.

"Why is that a question *you* have to answer?" Joss asked me.

And then I remembered the conclusion she finally reached

after the accident: *I didn't have to ask anymore why Elizabeth died, why Daddy died, why I didn't. The new question I was obsessed with was, "Okay, I lived—now what am I supposed to do with my life?"*

No matter how I got here, I'm alive. Now what do I do?

I am not trying anymore to pull my old self back together. I am not trying to be like Elizabeth, or not like Elizabeth. I am not trying to understand why I lived when the other clones died. I am just me. A new me.

We had to stay in Sanderfield, because my parents needed Myrlie to take care of them. It was so hard those first few weeks, getting on the school bus like any ordinary kid when I was anything but ordinary. The clumps of TV cameras outside the school didn't help. And even away from the cameras, I felt eyes following me all day long. The teachers were worse than the kids, because so many of them remembered Elizabeth.

But then a kid said to me in the lunch line one day, "My parents say I was a test-tube baby. I don't think anything could be weirder than *that.*"

And Mrs. Wade, the English teacher who's evidently been teaching in Sanderfield since the beginning of time, asked me to stay after class the same afternoon.

"I find that it's always a little disconcerting when I have identical twins in my classes," she said. "Do you understand the word, 'disconcerting'?"

"It means strange," I said. "Unsettling."

"Precisely," Mrs. Wade said. "I see you have a gift for language, just as your sister did. But I always tell identical twins that I, for one, understand that they are each individuals, that no two humans are ever exactly alike, and that I will judge each of them on his or her own merits. And I will do the same for you. Thank you. That is all."

As I walked out of school that day, I felt like I'd been given a gift. When Mrs. Wade and some of the others in Sanderfield look at me, they don't just see Elizabeth's clone or a scientific monster or an incredible news story or a chance for gossip. They see a human being.

They see me.

I am thirteen years old now—nearly thirteen and a half. And with each second that passes, I move further into territory Elizabeth never entered. Nobody knows what Elizabeth would have been like at fourteen, at fifteen, at sixteen. She is a ghost that will haunt me less and less, the older I get.

I am not glad that Elizabeth died. But I am glad that I'm alive.

It is spring now, and Joss has come up from St. Louis for the weekend.

"So . . . can we expect Bridgie to show up later this evening?" Myrlie teases.

"Come on, Mom," Joss says. "You know Bridgie was always Elizabeth's boyfriend, not mine."

"Speaking as Elizabeth's clone, I can assure you, Elizabeth would have lost interest in him by the time she was thirteen and a half," I say. "So you're welcome to him."

Joss rolls her eyes. But it's good to be able to joke about what used to horrify me. And I wouldn't mind going to a wedding in a year or so. Myrlie would be delighted to have a chance at grandchildren.

"Ta-da," my father says, walking around the corner of the house to join Myrlie, Joss, Mom, and me in the back yard. He's pushing a wheelbarrow. We all rush over to him to help steady what's inside the wheelbarrow: a new tree, its roots balled up in burlap.

It takes all five of us to place the tree in the ground, to pack dirt around its roots. My dad bought the biggest tree he could find.

"No sense getting a baby tree for some girl who's already half-grown," he said when we were planning this.

"What, am I going to end up being ten feet ten?" I joked.

"Who knows?" my dad answered, with a soft smile of his own.

Now I bend down to place a little wooden sign at the base of the tree. It reads, "Bethany Elaine Cole, Born November 2." There's no year, because I think of myself as having two November birthdays, almost exactly thirteen years apart. One was when I came into the world. And one was when I finally faced up to the whole truth about who I am.

"The tree is beautiful," my mother sighs happily. "Just like Bethany."

My tree right now is basically a collection of sticks with a few leaves budding out. Only a mother could call it beautiful. But come fall it will be as striking as Elizabeth's red maple—just in a different way. For my tree, I chose a ginkgo: a tree that's unique, with an unusual history. A tree that's survived against the odds.

Just like me.